Andrzej Sosnowski

Lodgings

Selected Poems
1987-2010

Translated from the Polish by Benjamin Paloff

OPEN LETTER
LITERARY TRANSLATIONS FROM THE UNIVERSITY OF ROCHESTER

Library of Congress Cataloging-in-Publication Data:

Sosnowski, Andrzej, 1959-
    [Poems. English. Selections]
    Lodgings : selected poems, 1987-2010 / Andrzej Sosnowski ;
translated from the Polish by Benjamin Paloff. — 1st ed.
        p. cm.
    ISBN-13: 978-1-934824-32-0 (pbk. : alk. paper)
    ISBN-10: 1-934824-32-1 (pbk. : alk. paper)
    I. Paloff, Benjamin. II. Title.

    PG7178.O8L66 2011
    891.8'517—dc22
                                    2010052054

Printed on acid-free paper in the United States of America.

Text set in Chaparral.

Design by N. J. Furl

Open Letter is the University of Rochester's nonprofit, literary translation press:
Lattimore Hall 411, Box 270082, Rochester, NY 14627

www.openletterbooks.org

Contents

TRANSLATOR'S NOTE

This book could well have been called *Music Boxes and Marienbads,*
the title of Andrzej Sosnowski's collected poems, published in 2009.
It might also have assumed the name *Inventory,* the last word of Sosnowski's poem "Errata," which is situated as the last poem of the
present volume. That we have opted for *Lodgings,* itself the title of
Sosnowski's 1997 collection, reflects both the poet's insistence on
inhabiting, however temporarily, an ever-shifting array of lyrical
modes and philosophical territories—an important frame for reading his work—as well as his admiration, shared by the translator,
for David Bowie, another stylistic chameleon, to whom these poems
sometimes refer.

Allusion is, in fact, one of the most important devices in Sosnowski's toolkit, in no small part because he scarcely distinguishes
between text and experience. That is, whether this poet's attention
passes from his ex-wife to James Schuyler or from Schuyler to his
ex-wife (the title of the longer "Poem for J. S." refers to both), literary antecedents and personal relationships overlap within his poetic
imagination. Though qualitatively distinct, they are equal as data
points that demand attention, confrontation, contemplation, and
ultimately navigation.

This helps account for the initial difficulties of reading Sosnowski's work. Indeed, Sosnowski's poems often read as intimate
addresses to an "invisible listener," as Helen Vendler has recently

suggested in regard to such poets as John Berryman and John Ashbery. Both of these poets have also been touchstone authors for Sosnowski; much of Ashbery's work available in Poland appears in Sosnowski's translation. Then there are Wallace Stevens and Frank O'Hara, Friedrich Hölderlin and Cyprian Norwid, Bocaccio, Martin Heidegger (whose *Being and Time* occasions the veiled polemic of *poemas,* Sosnowski's most recent book), and a large cast of French poets, novelists, and theorists, especially those dear to the New York School, from Raymond Roussel to Georges Perec to Alain Robbe-Grillet. All these inhabit the same lyric gestures as Greek myths, soccer stars, and old friends, not through the leveling of cultural value that we have otherwise come to expect from postmodern poetries, but through the simultaneous acknowledgement and instantiation of the demands every input makes on the individual consciousness. In this way, the beauty and challenge of Sosnowski's poems derive not from his elision of the rhetorical chains that might otherwise help us make sense of the whole—"this gadfly sense," he writes in "The Walk Ahead"—but from their *inclusiveness,* the practiced diligence that allows him to name as much as he can in the time that he has, and the discipline and restraint that permit that naming to tell its own story. Again, *inventory.* As he says in "What Is Poetry," itself a response to Ashbery's poem of the same name, "No need to regret delay, / for maybe it will sing?"

The poems here have been selected from nine of the collections Sosnowski published between 1992 and 2010 and are presented, with the exception of "Afterword" and "Errata," in their original order. *Nouvelles Impressions d'Amerique* (1994), a brilliant, book-length sequence of tightly interwoven prose poems based on Roussel's *Nouvelles Impressions d'Afrique,* did not lend itself to excerpt. Similarly, some of Sosnowski's long poems, notably the two title poems of his 1999 collection *Convoy. Opera,* proved inimical to the book that has emerged over the last three years. I hope to remedy these omissions in the future.

Several of these translations first appeared, often in different form, in a special chapbook issue of the *The Literary Review*. Others were published in *New European Poets* (Graywolf, 2008). My thanks go to Renée Ashley, Alissa Valles, Wayne Miller, and Kevin Prufer. I would also like to thank the Michigan Society of Fellows for time and resources, The Book Institute in Krakow for a two-month residency during which many of these translations were completed, as well as Jennifer Grotz, Grzegorz Jankowicz, Bill Martin, and Piotr Sommer for their encouragement of this project in its many stages. And to Andrzej, for life in Korea and life on Mars, thank you.

The rendering of Hölderlin at the end of "For Raymond Roussel" is lifted from Richard Sieburth's translation of "The Rhine," in *Hymns and Fragments* (Princeton, 1984). The two italicized lines near the end of "poemas," "the Rise of Capitalism Parallels . . . ," belong to John Ashbery's "Definition of Blue."

Benjamin Paloff
Ann Arbor
September 2010

Lodgings

Selected Poems
1987–2010

from
Life in Korea
(1992)

SUMMER 1987

And so it was that your death settled into my shadow
and leaned against me, breathed my thoughts.
I tore myself away, sought the noonday sun.
I was armed to the teeth with humor and vitamins.

I shrugged my shoulders and shook off my soul,
tore the black bandage, the black glow, from my memory.
You gave me panache. I ate fruit by the fistful.
Trace elements stood guard at my cells.

I went quickly, decisively, from one thing to the next.
I even jumped into marriage, humming epithalamia.
I even started working out: track, pushups, squat thrusts—
and exploited none for stupor before its time.

Those were days of stupor, and every night's sleep
was wild with the aura of delusions, the vertigo of desires,
like a great surge onto the surface of the earth,
rattling the body to enter its winter quarters.

And I just lost it, shed some altitude,
slipped out of step and rhythm, lost my breath—
fatal dromomania, crazy wanderlust—
not just from Bordeaux to Nürtingen, but always,

everywhere the earth beneath my feet so soft
I felt myself sinking up to the ankles.
And at night the bed was like a trap door.
It slipped out from under my body without a peep.

Later—the holds in my memory, peering into the window,
where the little girl in the building opposite
is smiling with a razor between her teeth.
I imagine her cool kisses.

TIME AND MONEY

The day stood still in the misty heat
The squeal of children in the cast-iron water
The rasp of beds making merry in the dry ports
We examine ourselves in the short-lived puddles
With lamplight horns on the crown of our heads
Our kisses flutter like slender bats
And each moves toward his own eyes
Toward cat stars on lunar discs
Or the little crystals of dew on spider webs

The illusion of chase will come a little later
When boredom shines its artificial light on the graying brain
And the clock slaps you on the back
And the seconds are like rookie narcs
Flickering on your legs like a jackpot of quarters
But then maybe there's something to accuse us of
Living with no greater effort
Two three weeks in the same color
Pointless profligacy

When you stretch out under somebody else's roof
Scruples taste like the sacrament

Years of eating in silence and stress
From the weakening grip of conscience on the throat
And the wind from the inferno's fifth canto dying down
And the fact that we have to hurt ourselves
If it's all to go singingly

THE WALK AHEAD

Did you deserve the highfalutin fiction
of this life *sans* fact, this gadfly sense?
The megaphones at dusk announce secrets,
words of mountains over which no sun will break,
and in the mounting din you catch the orchestras
of carnival processions: jugglers and clowns
move into the main arteries, bells and cymbals
ring like a hail of mayflies. And the heart
does an about-face, and the mind breaks
ranks as the world darkens in your eyes,
which then take flight, flustered, nestle
beneath their lids, or hide under the bushes
of your brows, because enough already, enough.
When am I going to stop falling into these worlds?
When you rein it in and start living hand-to-mouth,
when you give these crippled landscapes a try, look out the corner
of your eye, collect the scraps of roadside business,
find the point and from that point on denature
your post. Then you can take a walk
with pockets full of cash and perfumed handkerchiefs,
just in case. And now you step into evening
as if onto the high road, and in the darkness the air
is growing thick with phantoms: their voices pulsate
like frogs croaking, the tremendous hymn of mosquitoes.

LIFE IN KOREA

It may be high time to look for a good one,
maybe they won't press you to the wall, maybe you won't
be dumbstruck, mouth frozen with shame, tripping
over yourself to apologize for your anachronism. Just a thought:
once again your quick words forecast
a scorching hot harvest and your rapture at sunset,
when the dancing begins, the intoxicating
anticipation of these trite love affairs,
as refreshing as the crab apple
you casually pluck as you pass through the orchard,
bite into, and throw away. And life is a similarly, suddenly
pleasurable stretch, a patronizing
yawn at the sun: So you're here too,
old chum? And you, my fine feathered friends?
Indeed. I propose rituals and prayers,
and I'm worried. May they work out for you,
may you not pass out on the tracks, upon which the days
thunder by in shiny sleepers,
and the nights stand still in the freight cars
beneath the signal. The intellect dozes a little,
the senses have their turn, and again I'm seized
by the lovely things of this world: apples, water, milk,
purest air. And once you get it,
that you haven't earned these or any other
fifteen minutes, you can have a drink,
smash your world to pieces, and at long last
think it over.

POEM FOR YOUR DAUGHTER

You're wrong to think I won't stray from the path,
if you understand path to mean the morning drill, the rock's sleep,
because someone's eyes will launch sleep's dugout from shore,
and I'll come to in the reeds or on the open sea.
I have a knack for these things. The river,
of course, only goes one way, and if tomorrow
I sit at the edge of the sea like a daydreaming ass and await
the mysteries, it's only because I got carried away.
Blame it on the crosscurrent.

Tonight I fell in love with your daughter again,
though I haven't seen her in four years. In my sleep
I called her sister, but what's the logic or sense in that?
She was in a plastic red sailing hat and standing
on the riverbank, surrounded by cats
with pupils like green watch dials—the ricochet
of thinking about time, the years that have separated us.
I've had it up to here with time dogging me in my sleep.

But I also have cause for unconcealed joy, that she
is not my daughter, nor you my wife, nor my sister
(you would be her mother), etc. It's all physically
impossible. Or not. Whatever. Maybe another time

I'll wake up on the rocks.

MILLENNIUM

It's the millennium. It's everywhere and always
processions of girls in white and boys in blue
through golden cities, smiling into the empty sky.
On the seventh day the rains stopped; the lines started.
Gray clouds peeled down like musical wallpaper.
In the downpour of songs, standing right next to you,
observing the people bound in cords of slogans,
I'm wondering whether what we're really in line for
is some luck, destiny cut into thousands
of colorful cards, all of it make-believe,
like the "Hallelujah" billboards on the projects
or the banners announcing joy and a harvest of meaning. And you?
"Like those sleepy Indians among the statues,
passed out on the terraces of unkempt temples,
we discover in the flash of cameras that history's a show,
diamond dust on the shoes of a great actor."
That's all she says. Not another word, nothing,
no asking about what to do under these new conditions,
no request for expertise. Because everyone
is expecting obscenity, some kind of "think about it
and die," or declensions, through the senses, through all
the ifs, and in what, and with whom, and what then. So sure,
take the first flight to Berdichev or Barvistan—
that's where you'll find me.

AUTUMN

They, too, cross the line, the mayor and the elite,
sending letters full of big promises
of a life so staggering that the glare over the tracks
plays like a music box, and somebody laughs through his nose
when the wind scatters the leaves and exposes the blood
that's concealed the gold of autumn. And we feel like crying,
for we suffer modestly among noteworthy victims.
But somebody explains to someone that he lives voraciously,
leaping from night into onrushing mornings,
and somebody stifles his groans in the evening
by putting on an ironic smile like a double-breasted suit.
And it's only in autumn that you can know the ideoplastics
of sleep, which arise from mounds of air:
in girum imus nocte et consumimur igni
(we circle around at night and are consumed by fire).

DEATH OF AN UNFORMED MAN

It's yours: go ahead and smile
at the need to simplify, stop the body
while rousing the soul, for this dizziness
is not what it used to be, not the hard dreams of winter,
like rocketing off a mammoth ski jump,
nor spring's momentum: the flare, a dancer's sash
shooting into the dark, you gliding after it
like you're on a waterslide, straight into pools of summer.
How long can you wander the line?
Shadow-boxer, one hard hit and you're head
over heels into interstellar space, the world's whisper
behind you like an avalanche out of breath.

And what now, as lonely as a finger on ice, once
you've abandoned what causes you'd no cause to take up?
Our talk sounded like "yeah, yeah," in good times, and in bad,
"whatever, whenever." And it keeps getting worse:
you hang around in the dirt by the bridge into town,
casting pebbles like a gentleman caller no one's called;
you look at a clear sky and reminisce about clouds,
tempests of long-past causes and thunderous meanings.
And at night the world takes in your light, and so what,
just the moths' tapping against the pane and a cricket
like someone walking in buckled shoes.
I'd like to fall victim to whatever intrigue they have.

WHAT IS POETRY

Sure, it's no strategy for survival,
nothing to live on. Your obstinacy is laughable
as you recall the enchanted lakes,
the rustling woods and hushed caverns
where a voice echoes out vividly, and has for centuries.
Sibyls? What matters is leaves, then maybe the rhyme
of *voice* and *choice*, since voices press against the world,
and choice is that which does not entrust names
to leaves. Just you try to catch them! Try
to touch the ground and fly farther,
like a flat stone over water—how many times?
Five, twelve? A sequence of poems and reflections,
a sequence of leaves, and anyway all the stones and leaves
lie one beside the other according to an ancient order,
their forms unclear. Then there's the cavern
or the teeny room. But that gust!
The draft as you open the door, and the wind
disperses the leaves, and the world rears up,
and the words come like a sprinkling of confetti.
But don't give us the stinkeye, don't head out
a sourpuss, not yet. No need to regret delay,
for maybe it will sing? Perhaps it will suddenly say
what people and wars are like, travels and travails,
how things stand, what news?

THREE POEMS FROM THE NEAR NORTH

Huntsville

La sexe est sombre, et, Henri Parisot,
parce que la poésie l'est encore plus.
—Antonin Artaud

The days don't amount to much: groceries, affronts,
and that coarse openness in the little cardboard houses,
without shutters, curtains, drapes, or blinds,
so that you know too much and suffer the sense
of participating in everybody's confession to everybody else.
Everywhere here it's cliff, boredom, and exposure,
a plateau of ennui and belletristic moods:
you're free to answer any question posed by anyone,
anytime, anywhere. And our world
unfolds into tedious rhythmic passages
strewn haphazardly in all directions—
a wave, whine of a loon, thunder, footsteps, breath—
as if some demiurge were sitting on a pebble beach
and skipping stones through the universe with a concentration
worthy of better things. But will any of this
become a part of our dying? Because I think
that death is like that lake set upright in air,
all hidden in reddish fog, the bangs of light.
And now it's already night. And nights are more
interesting, they mount pictures, the moon
like a lemon wedge perched on the edge of the glass
suddenly falls into the fog, and one cardboard house looks

like a tall pina colada on snow. And you can hear the cricket's
"my-oh-my" harsh critique, you can hear every breath,
and you have to keep doing everything as though on the sly,
a finger to somebody's lips, your teeth
to your own wrist, because the night, like love, must be
as quiet and empty as the Baptists' beach on Sunday.
But even the night is theirs, for the aurora borealis,
that crown, bridgehead, or spur of light
in night's river (though for me it's rather a frosted glass,
or else a hand on night's warm forehead), is suggestive enough
for them to spraypaint the cliffs
about the judgment soon to come, to write
with a finger on a filthy car that Jesus died
for our sins. And on every lawn:
my presence shall go with thee. Indeed,

the only thing we're not used to are those morning times
when the laughter dies down and the games peter out, subversive
fun—sorry about making Parcheesi out of shoots and ladders,
like seriousness out of irony. And I remember the white of salt
on lips, morning desire, cognizance of a lack
that, once we were aware of it, became a secret,
like that night butterfly, a moth as big as a child's hand,
as if from dyed suede, the period at the end of night—
an emblem of sleep, or else the magic initial
that opens an illuminated manuscript
whose contents we will never know.

•

Wild Water Kingdom

But these huge water slides, such a lovely
gift to laughter and, in a certain sense, from laughter, too.
No inhibitions here. More than anything else, *déshabille*;
everyone's practically naked, and no one keeps straight,
and if they keep straight, it's to lie prostrate
and drop, to fall down laughing, lie down
laughing and fly, with dizzying velocity,
wound-up by laughter, into an explosion of water,
like the salvo of laughter at the end
of a joke played on posture and decorum. Here it is,
perpetuum mobile, alchemy of motion for the body,
because even after a hard night, after the black sabbath, all it takes
is two hours to get back all your potency and *raison,*
without even having to throw yourself down the vertical
drop or fly through the azure tube, but maybe just
floating down the Lazy River or quivering with delight
in a hot jacuzzi. And next they ring the coming wave
(which rises in a windowless building), whose rhythm recalls
the eternity that spurs you to go on sliding,
as if through the sky-blue slide of time or the taut
rubber stretched across the calves of the two lifeguards
standing at the pool's edge. Here are the megaphones
(everything is appearance, the joy of the moment,
the monument on fire, delight in falling)
and the din, and those shouts of *whoa* and *oh boy* from all sides,
bodies quick as silver and pretty nymphettes
so absorbed in themselves and still always
finding the right moment to bathe the men
in a not-quite-innocent gaze in which something
is shimmering, the quick shadow of a smile,

the foretaste of Virginia's laugh, which Paul will sense
like an ice cube trembling on his belly. And I wish
to sink into this *folie lucide*, I want to know
vertige de l'hyperbole, commotio

vel fluctus. There's the constant flow of water,
the rush, theoretically no ground beneath your feet,
though this is apparently just "in theory," so that even here
you can balance—on ribbons of water, in a snowstorm?
But you're not allowed to go head-first. It's the legs
that lead, and what arouses delight
is an exaultation of the legs so carnivalesque
(the head dragged behind like a laughing toy),
especially in so blatantly comic a setting,
among synthetic forms, neither masculine, nor feminine,
awash in hectoliters of heraclitian water
pouring in all directions like the metaphor
of fluids circulating in Swedenborg's angel.
And the whole thing flips over into a kind of allegory.
In the flow of water see a parody of all the tears
in the world streaming together, see in this system
of blue waterfalls a crown of branches
intertwined like serpents, a wondrously
grotesque version of a mythic tree,
nature outsmarted in the act of allegory,
which apes the garden of earthly delights
as well as the garden of sciences with these hyperboles,
parabolas, these sine waves of pleasure,
erudite spirals of laughter. And I have no idea
whether it all ends happily or in madness,
the vegetable dignity of joy or convulsions of laughter,
because relations can change, but exile
is always the same. Are you afraid, little girl? At night

these slides shimmer in the water's blue light
under a black sky, and we fly off
the rainbow's arcs as though off the negatives
of underexposed feelings, and each has his own laugh
that cuts through space like a comet's foamy tail,
like a flower that adorns the night with the solitude
of that heady light. And we are moving
in opposite directions, inevitably, dropping, *down
we go*. And that's fine by me.

•

All That Jazz

Now calling 666.
—in the waiting room

God bless the accelerations. When the stars descend
they lock facial features, darken smiles, and the wastes
get back into the formation broken by day,
which gave your heart something to murmur about:
the sun's needle sews the confusion that moves you,
which sight-reads the music within us for dying voices
each is like a path to the edge of dialect's canvas.

If you want to get going, shift the beat
from the louder parts of the bar to the muted ones, and
consider this: the design is stripped to its fibers,
to the dust of feeling, to its listening stations, so try to thwart
the second between the instruments' stitches, that it might let
syntax in and a new language to cast a thick pattern
over the blind map of emotions, like hail, and so lightening-fast

as to dampen the rustle of timpani and harps, though the undertone
must remain, thereby to quicken the stream
of syncopation, fast as the flow of silence falling on those
who've been struck dumb with happiness. And things
will flash through you fully illuminated
and as free of meaning as the day upon whose hillsides
you caught expansive views of the future.

Still, you should start by breaking the seals
on the books of phantoms of common storylines,
so that you can encompass their grace, write out their parts,
sprain the tendons of sense. Rush everything
that is slave to duration. Love,
but test that love daily with dreams as strong
as wormwood tea and new music.

from
A Season in Hel
(1994)

POETRY DEGREE ZERO

Maybe that's what it takes for someone to love you,
the voice hung in the tunnel. But the thought
reverberated overhead through the noise of switches,
and our bodies were enveloped in the spacesuit
of sleep, we picked up speed and the heart
rocked in the throat like a tear,
as the container, the hangars, the neon lights,
the bleeding of detail in darkened eyes
shone behind us like the tail of a comet—
some god was working at all hours.
"We're all hot for these books," X screamed, and
I: "Isn't somebody going to ask me for a foreword
to the phonebook for this town?" And Z: "An
afterword, maybe." And will no one discover
us, light at this latitude, like
light's haste in the tunnel, the oval
of the little lamp on its unmarked grave?
At the end of the light there's a tunnel.

FOUNDING A CERTAIN COLONY

Guard posts, patrols, decrees, until finally
the locals arrived, just to make sure nothing
of theirs got moved! And we: Not so fast! With this
cemetery to the south, to disperse more or less
among the garden plots at the edge of town, break through
the spacious arteries and tunnels, erect
an elevated train, excavate canals and grant passage
to motor boats, ferries, hydrofoils, and to hell
with souvenirs: Let the bulldozers' silhouettes
show up on the blueprints, he said
(laying his match on the city map), this is where
we'll have our theater of operations. And later?
Release the fog. At dusk, only a boy's laughter
in the blind courtyard will answer the color
of time, which abandoned them while
asking for a space they hadn't dreamt of.

FOUNDING ANOTHER COLONY

And we'll have to furnish them with news
media, enigmatic surveys, reports
on the number of steps the ballerina took
at the casting call, and ethereal shots
of Antarctic snow, a flash of butterfly
wings in the dust of an Andean waterfall,
non-stop, live, and without commentary.
And the same old station breaks. And quality?
Has the art of dying gone out of style?
No initials. Those who don't like it are free
to pass single-file through foreign territory,
seeking adventures not on the schedule.

CV

And in the split second between him and me
someone else from the aforementioned photo moves
in identical air, joins in the music
ahead by half a second, but a shadow
slower, though the snap of the shutter
opens a gray time for us both.

It doesn't matter whether I'm engrossed or forgetting
myself. Doesn't matter if I'm asleep or sitting in front of the TV,
blasted by water and mud, in the rustle of leaves
opposite this hell or another.
Fall sure is inspiring.
You struggle to catch a free hand
and draw it to your warm side.

But the rhyme doesn't work, there being but one hand in that world.
Two little flames light cigarettes,
but the hand holding the match, alone,
the one that is writing, is already on the other side.
Even when it's into a gray autumn morning
we set off into perfect visibility.

A SEASON IN HEL

Banquo: It will be rain to-night.
1st Murderer: Let it come down.

We're late entering summer; let's leave
our watches on the beach. Time, too,
has its weather. For example, in a minute
your sunny signet will vanish into the wet sand,
setting in the foot-flood of this swarthy clan.
And the humidity might dream its own dream of the museum,
spinning out along the springs and stones
and steaming beneath its golden envelope
to the very edge of the sea and time.

Every night I drink half a liter with my lady.
Dressed the same for a date, the dumps, and for work,
at times we really do seem temporary,
the phosphorescent points on the peninsula's
minute hand on the sea's dial. And so great
is her need for living space, while we
have our hearts in our packs and just clear
the forest of old fortifications, the fascine fences,
letting time slip with a light foot
slipped into sand.

That's how they clear the dunes to serve time.
You happen to the sun, if not to the clouds,
though quite rarely, so that you carry yourself like a mystery,
your shoe stamping out time like a butt in the sand.

And sometimes, with a lighthouse to our lips,
we turn the light away and broadcast ourselves in the morning,
in unaddressed envelopes. And it rains.
Motionless breakers rise above us.
The news media will say nothing about how our eyes
met, though it proved unusually consequential.

TANNHÄUSER

My laughter died under the bed; perhaps at night
it will jump down the throat of your dreams or lightly
whip your pulse and get a couple of words out of you,
"clip-clop," "bump-bump"? But isn't sound
too heavy? Wouldn't it be better if it were a wave
of light? A reflection in dark glasses,
a rainbow on officer's boots, a stain of warmth
on a leather jacket—oh, just to be
the evening spark in your eye, to brush
against the edge of a tear, to shimmer on the blade
of the alarm clock's hand and alight
in the lighter you're bringing to your lips!
To shine like a prodrome in the pupil and be
so fast, faster than a flash
of desire beneath the eyelid! And so to live in the flutter
of eyelashes, and finally to settle in the voice—the shadow
of light? But first, only the echo
mulling around your sleep like a gangster's flashlight,
and just at daybreak a sound, like a case,
of the whisper of megaphones at the end
of the line, somewhere on your border, and to live
in your borderlands, till you hear the breath,
the touch of finger to lips, and come out,
standing straight in the green flames.

A SONG FOR EUROPE

A rainbow? Fourteen years since anyone's seen one,
which means "the end of the world," or something like that.
Don't hunker in a bunker. When love is most literally
a magic that divides life into pleasure and loss, as a mermaid
trims memory before the air-raid of reminiscence,
we are in Germany, on the border with France.
A dream arises about intercontinental war.
The nocturnal emissions of factories, embers, dissonance,
and the style of this history is so elusive you have to drive
the poem down this track, then that one, if it's to make it
into the hands of its unknown addressee.

It was never like that. Yes it was.
Will you be? A strange tryst—the emerald
around your neck and the shadow on your eyes—a smile,
or a black armband for the passing of a word?
An emerald, that you might not stare
into the death within you? That the poem might approach
you like a shadow and cover your eyes, this
poem—a shadow cast over truth, from the depths
of a tear, a splinter of light, the spot of glass
that concludes the conversation of broken mirrors?

Be this glass when it's all over, in the silence of *all clear*.
Weren't we cruel, embarking so lightly
on this dark life, not a word
when you pulled the ground out from under me,
and the sky broke down in snow? Love
is not this word, nor any other.
The poem declares it like blitzkrieg.

THE END OF THE CENTURY

Nothing to get upset about: our world is nothing if not fetching. Something exceptional must have happened that fine day when it stopped drizzling early in the morning, and the clouds sat at the edge of the sky like snow on the road's shoulder, like the insignificant margin of our most auspicious hours. We took a little more of the air, stretched out, looked around; was there anyone who was not at that moment congratulating himself on the bright autumn that had finally come, fully equipped, with its cool sun, elongated shadows, and Indian summer? It seemed as if everyone were greeting each other with some secret sign, as if they'd wanted to say that the test was over, though we should hold off jumping for joy, because the results, while promising, are not yet in. The women smiled playfully at any gaze they chanced upon, and the warm feelings of men, full of tact and humor, stirred, as though kindness were a wonderful joke you had to repeat aloud and in your memory from one morning to the next. No doubt, in the depth of his soul everyone had a strong feeling that the days of wisdom, of quiet conversations beneath the red maples, had arrived, time for reminiscence and laughter at café tables, and secrets confessed between two sips of coffee, when the eternity of the early afternoon seems to concentrate within itself the finest essences of all the unusual things you can live through and whose legendary existence we've half-hidden in the darkness of mystery. And weren't we excited to discover, somewhere at the bottom of these golden hours, the sweet certainty of adulthood, which gave us leave to lose ourselves in the pleasure of unconditional forgiveness for all the misdeeds that had cut us to the quick, and that, after all, testify to the generosity of our common nature? The most beautiful confidences coursed throughout the day, and everywhere you could hear voices, trembling and happy, for what you'd once driven into the Cimmerian regions of your conscience suddenly became like autumn fruit, juicy and full of sweetness, which you have to share with your closest friends in a moment of youthful excess. Love, adulthood, the women repeated, and they gave the men quick, amorous glances, laughing at all the little stories of infidelities committed those many years ago with chicks whose names were lost to the dusty archive of the heart, of the body. And isn't it true that, strictly speaking, betrayal is never betrayal if it doesn't lead to a habit of the soul, or of the nerves, or else isn't it merely a trifle on the surface of the skin, a trivial delight we allow ourselves, only then to be bound more powerfully to the one our unerring heart has truly chosen? Few can resist the temptation of little pleasures and immediate satisfaction, but they are innocent, the men were arguing, and the women nodded and gave back in kind, with tales of crazy nights on business trips, at conferences, about actors they knew, for whom they would have done anything if things had gone a little differently. There was an extraordinary atmosphere of dreams fulfilled, of the greatest good luck, as if time had reached a limit and stopped, satisfied, in the rain of benedictions pouring down on the world like the golden mist of the setting sun. "Is life a concert of well-wishing?" the most miserable among us were asking, spending their evenings in bars where inveterate smokers sang of sweet tobacco and talked, intense and joyful, late into the night with aficionados of something stronger, for isn't it true that only an organism plagued by a spiritual tension brought on by an unconscious sense of guilt succumbs to partial or complete destruction in the grip of addiction? Complete assent, carefree submission, surrender of mind and body to the wonderments of smoke and liquor allows us to enjoy our health in a slightly altered dimension, and indeed the sole misfortune is a conscience that feeds on false moral and medical knowledge. And we could hear laughter and singing, and the whole city was experiencing one of those rare moments of liberation familiar to all cities that have survived the misfortune of war and occupation. They spoke of the increase in spirit and endless flights, of building new bridges and forging friendships, of the lungs' blessed apathy and the body's resignation, of the sweetness of smoke that knocked the nerves down a peg or three, of the boiling in the throat and the relief that a couple drops of liquor brought, and again of the whoosh of smoke in the bronchi, of the betrayal and love of it all, of love. Truly, we were witnesses to the end of philosophy that Heidegger had predicted. The old-timers, sensing that each of us would be trying to get some business going in the near future, shared their advice with the impatient youth, starting with the observation that centuries of philosophers' effort had gone into convincing people that life isn't so easy. Not your neighbor's thighs, nor clever bookkeeping, nor the athlete's laurels, nor the makeup of fame on the silver screen, nor the dog's wet nose by the crackling fireplace, drowning out the swish of palm trees and the ocean. But the people preferred to speculate about the soccer star's salary, about the miraculous child of two queers or the genius horse, and right they were, the old-timers solemnly declared, for hasn't Hollywood given us plenty of examples of the tremendous advances and romances of individuals who were basically worthless and not too sharp, but who nevertheless, with a little good old-fashioned elbow grease, triumphantly laid the groundwork for today's holiday of metaphysical reconciliation? Had not the factories of dreams always announced, with a glimmer of hope, that the fundamentally simple, prefabricated components of happiness, known to man since the dawn of history, ultimately lend themselves to being arranged into a kind of shared home, so simply and nobly constructed that the very notion of the need to defend its holy walls before the philosophers' sarcasm aroused the uncontrollable laughter of generations? But then perhaps the neighbor's thighs, they asked treacherously, and right away they added, with greater wisdom and sobriety, with that darkness of the eyes with which years of study and experience washes our pupils: work at one's trade, a warm corner, a bit of scratch. Conferences and delegations, tourism and sports, tolerance, understanding, conscientiousness, as well as freedom of association, faith in the ideals of youth, the independence of the judiciary, punctuality, respect for one's superiors, the ability to take full advantage of the situation as it arises, business sense and industriousness, ruthlessness and refinement of manner, lack of sexual hang-ups, courage and an uncompromising outlook, sticktoitiveness, goodness—and then a modicum of something inexpressible and mystical, faith in something enduring and indestructible, yet realizable in the sphere of the ideal values that the best of us have always seen there, the old-timers smiled, indicating the pink-hued horizon, there where everything was made so simple and practical that there was really nothing left to do but work a bit on oneself, especially as it's looking to be a fantastic day, and it's time to rub your eyes in the sad cafés, the factories of dreams, the quaint little houses in the country.

AND OTHER TALES

not a whit more of definitions
of a diagram of work the factory the end the sun
and moving on to our next item
all-nighter customer no smoking please pass
the dream exam just before midnight
the moon awoke like a wolf
in my face and veered left and right
garlanding the faces of the graduating class
but these ideograms trip me up professor
the diagram of work the factory the end the sun
come back

we don't have to spend much time on this teach
a split second and we got it appreciate
the famous silence stitched with the gold of legends
mute asyndeton through the downtown artery
those who are willing and captive
in nameless details
in homelessness laughter the whisper incarnate
of the voice beyond the spaces in musical notation
we try so hard to pass over language in silence
but the story can make us
soon and without much trouble
want to wrap up
soon and without much trouble
the diagram of work the factory the end the sun
in the dark eyes of this schoolgirl
effort of the one civilization
that has outlived its god
and other tales

KILLARNEY

Let's say, the angle of refraction of bodies: does it not increase
under the eyes of loved ones? And in the warm breath
that condenses around a nominative, a pronoun, the contrail
of a lost plane? Aren't your ears filled
with the path's confusing footfalls, aren't you waiting
for the alarm, the rattle and bang of the tongue at the sound
of just a hint of rhythm in those fading footsteps, the attack
of fine old histories—that the morning role call
(everyone accounted for) might, under threat of speech,
catch it all in its crosshairs,
its locative, its instrumental, its polite dialect,
but for the grace of God? Though the heart's bug
hasn't gone dead, and the secret agents
are moved by the same easy songs.

ASLEEP AND NOT SO MUCH

And it might have seemed we were on our way
to some brilliant picnic, that the motors were playing, dreams
cutting across the horizon, and the highway's point
stitched the ribbon of sky with a quiver of lightning,
as the hair of our women sang on the wind,
frozen like harp strings against the blue.
After such knowledge, what enchantment? The beautiful
women are no longer formerly our women—
they wandered the stairs sobbing, not sliding
down the banister: one must get lost
and laugh sweetly in darkness,
drifting into orgasm as the night bell rings,
for its world has crashed into the sky's windshield
and is a dry stain on the sky's enormous windshield.

Of course, if we had taken a hot-air balloon
we could have cast roses on the wind and made love to the women.
But all we had was words, not even our own words,
extinguished in the melancholy of autumn evenings,
when the days walk down the lane toward winter, and the sky
is as sharp as a blue scalpel slicing through the fundus
of the eye—the bottom of our eyes, but not the bottom of us,
gushing the blood of artesian slides
from the anticlines of awkward dialects.
After such knowledge, what satiety?
I heard—what?—night workers?
In the oneiric aura of a new language, its music
an anonymous word's worth wiser than our own,
they penetrated my eye like nobody, my love,
who always drifts away in a dither as I'm counting sheep.

FOR CHILDREN

And the princess turns into a hag, and the prince
flees to the south, screaming bloody murder? Spit it out
and come here. That lift of the eyebrow, your clever whistle—
will it be enough to lay the sandbag
in the gliding gondola of our stroll
through the day's green decline, through a city
so unconscious of its transformation into fairytale
that nightfall still has nothing to do with anyone
but the volley of balls on the courts and swings screeching
on the evening playgrounds? Like the two shadows
from the picture at the end of the book, and whistling,
through the stretch between anywhere and nowhere,
holding hands. The silly dolphins
that border the figure of a goddess risen from the waves,
in the light of a great building, and spitting
water—aren't they like applause
for a glimmering star? But shh, you say,
you want to watch. They're totally nuts!
You who break away from the pack by the fountain,
you who enter the pool's basin denuded
and rub up against the moist statue until the spasm
on its stone buttocks! Is that ecstasy's
inscription? Graffiti in the eyes
of the sorry rabble, who must feel
that certain files can only be signed in blood?
As I shall do presently.

FOR RAYMOND ROUSSEL

Nobody knows how it will work: a forty-year-old
hires a lackey to take his place while he
stays home and writes, reads dictionaries, writes, fifteen
hours a day: "my soul is a strange factory."
During regular breaks he smokes opium and makes a mad dash
around the globe: Africa, America, China,
Australia, Japan, Tahiti (in Peking
he didn't once leave the hotel), he travels
Europe in a roulotte of his own ingenious design, complete
with office, kitchen, bathroom, and servant's quarters. He never
leaves the roulotte. For his work
"can contain nothing of reality, nothing observed,"
only structures completely imagined.

"I would choose two nearly identical words, such as *billard* [billiard
table] and *pillard* [plunderer]. First I looked for words connected with
billard, but I always chose the ones with a more distant meaning.
Thus the word *queue* [a pool cue; the train of a dress] furnished me
with the train of King Talou. A billiard cue often has its owner's
chiffre [monogram], and thus the *chiffre* [code] on the royal train."

At nineteen he is already writing day and night, he draws
the shades that the sunlight on the text not blind Paris.
("The glare could reach all the way to China.") The nibs glow,
a star falls on his brow, his halo pulses like blood: "*formidable
euphorie,* I felt what Tannhäuser felt at Venusberg." He eats
once every three days with the same pedantry (22 courses
in fifteen hours) with which he changes his clothes: collars

go to the cleaners after every use, suits
are worn fifteen times. His bulldog smokes a pipe
expertly. As a novelty he brings an electric heater
back from India, he installs a window
in his mother's casket, "to conduct minor experiments."

R.'s deeds also emerge from secret combinations of words:
biography is grammar. "In the not-distant future
even my way of playing tag
will be universally acknowledged."

"I would connect one word with another using the preposition *à* [to,
on, with, in, by, etc.]. Example: 1) *Roue* [wheel] *à caoutchouc* [rubber].
2) *Roue* [cocky] *à caoutchouc* [rubber tree]. Thus the rubber tree on
the round Trophy Square where Talou cockily placed his foot on his
opponent's torso."

Nothing, then, is accidental, though everything
is arbitrary. The initiative rests entirely
with the words, for among all our dreams
the most beautiful are word-dreams that bloom
like Japanese flowers on water: wasn't the author of *Albatross
beau de l'air*? Who but the Surrealists
could love such games? "On the ruins of Balbec
Gilbert bangs the famous uneven sistrum
of the great poet Missir" (he was Proust's neighbor),
on the ruins of imagining his own fame R. systematically
takes barbiturates in predetermined series
(Somnothyril, Soneryl, Rutonal, Declonol, Veriane),
over 40 pills daily (Mme. Dufrène notes the effects
on a scale from *sans euphorie* to *euphorie*

très grande). He shoots opium and drinks, plays
chess fanatically (Tartakower writes three studies
of his endgames), composes his *Nouvelles
Impressions d'Afrique*, and in a certain respect
Europe dreams its loveliest dream in him, in this final *pas*
unburdened of speech: Mussolini visits his roulotte
and wipes his eyes. And here we have the diamond bathtub
and an earthworm playing the zither. And these
are the famous calf-lung rails. But how?

"Here's how: 1) *mou* [wimp] à *raille* [by which I meant school kids
making fun of a lazy classmate). 2) *mou* [lungs] à *raille* [rail]."

It's unclear when he started working
on his death. In 1931 he sits down to *How I Wrote
Certain of My Books*, complains that his only successes
were songs sung in salons
and sketches in which he imitated actors, commoners,
and God. "It was an enormous success."
It's unclear what sequence of signs
would bring him to Palermo, what syntax
would settle him into the Hotel Grande Albergo e delle Palme,
where Wagner wrote *Parsifal*. Full of sorrow, on the 13th
of July (Bastille Day's Eve) he takes his usual dose of drugs,
sits at the window, watches the festival honoring Saint Rosalia
and a Balbo squadron (9:30, a display of allegorical lights
on the boats and barges in front of the Foro Umberto: "a reiter
trots across the sky, bowing to an invisible
Amazon"). Whatever—commands, artificial fires—
Mme. Dufrène doesn't know when he locks the door
between their rooms (something he never did), when he opens

the door to the hall, when he drags the heavy straw mattress
against the locked door. In the morning
his body is resting on that mattress, his right arm
outstretched, his index finger
pointing toward the locked door.

("A riddle," says Hölderlin, "the pure of source.")

POMONA AND VERTUMNUS

The stained glass wanton, the frescoes lecherous,
ivy ironclad on the first-floor windows—
Don't think, Pomona, that I've made up this world
or, Vertumnus, the spans of your reveries.

Ivy ironclad on the first-floor windows
tells us that children have occupied the city.
And, Vertumnus, the spans of your reveries
are like the city smiling at the end of the street.

They tell us that children have occupied the city.
The fates of these children arouse no interest.
They're like the city smiling at the end of the street
on a sun-scorched, would-be rainy day.

The fates of these children arouse no interest.
Perhaps these children's children will already be gone
on a sun-scorched, would-be rainy day,
when time will somersault and night will fall.

Perhaps these children's children will already be gone
after the end of history on this colorful planet,
when time will somersault and night will fall
and there'll be naughty night-vision games all around.

After the end of history on this colorful planet
they'll have a perfect view of the cathedral spire,
and there'll be naughty night-vision games all around
in the shadow the syringe casts on the tunnel wall.

They'll have a perfect view of the cathedral spire,
the stained glass wanton, the frescoes lecherous
in the shadow the syringe casts on the tunnel wall.
Don't think, Pomona, that I've made up this world.

OFF SEASON

The sea's frozen, ice clear to the horizon. Hills of sand, of water mixed with sand so perfectly that the globules of this new matter have the consistency of firni, they point out where the breaker's been, and right behind them a frozen sheet rolls out, a cold, open hand furrowed with wavy lines, crests, plumes of snow: a wispy portrait of air in the momentary collision of wind and water-dust, an alphabet of meanings fleeing past the horizon and repeated in unending vibrations, lifeless inferences. I'm thinking of the poverty of Venice. Casting no shadow, I step into the heart of it, listening to the crunch of ice beneath my feet. But when I stop there will be extraordinary quiet surrounded by the whisper of steaming snow, of falling crests and friezes more delicate than ash. Here and there the sheet breaks, brisk as lightening, the contours of the floe in patches, outlines of decay. And I imagine one could take this whole for a jig-saw puzzle, sit and wait for the water to wash away the pattern, the madness of frost, till it sinks, slowly, to the bottom.

You do not hear me upstairs—or is that the sky? Too white not to look at, too quiet to hear a word. I venture a touch, lying down on the snow: I run my fingers on the wispy summits, the icy geysers, efflorescence of frost, coronas. The sky is reflected in this . . . mirror . . . so completely that as I am lying on my back the clouds seem to pass through me like sand through an hourglass and, stiffening, freezing in ribbons of snow, lay themselves out in lines of print, soon to tremble at the sun's touch. A few more shifts of the body, and the sea is like the vault of a white grotto, where I am hanging like a bat, and where the sky hangs beneath it like a sea.

And at night—I'm staying the night—the rumble and scrape of the ice, creaking, boom, as if playing on ship cables, some serious effort—for what? to shift something? for the moon? for another satellite? to arrange those snow-covered crests into a smile? a secret smile, since no one is watching? And when there really is no one else watching, I see the eddy, the surf, a blizzard of forms: shadow without a head, snakes coiled into nooses, the deranged dance of berserkers, of archons.

from
Lodgings
(1997)

CLOSE READING

So the fire forced us into the middle of the road;
the clapper will give us the signal any minute.
Come back, we gushed, and rushed onward, and now
run for it, and down the hill, like water on a millwheel
out of breath, out of earth, if only to have something
to dream of. It's as easy as a song,

so much heart, such a move. But was it so
polished, and apparently polychromatic,
the thread of days, calendar pages
shining like exotic postage stamps
in an album—was this our fuse, my cockatrice?
I'm afraid we have the fuses right here.

I'm afraid, sir, we have a problem.
Strike of the match. Hyena laugh, and the light
blows up in your face. Boom. The crowd
goes wild. The hero
departs in an awful light,
looking over the ruins of empire.

There is a glow in the eyes of his beloved.

And we are shining with absence, neon lights
in an untidy aquarium. That sound,
that drone—when did you start hearing it
beneath the famous lullaby, or perhaps you took it

from on high that the background doesn't matter? And yet
even in sleep you leave traces, and only
some of them are entirely clear, like something
that doesn't remind us of, or is not itself, blood.

WARSZAWA

Yesterday, after the paper, they were giving out a new hymn, actually
a two-for-one mazurka and dream cake in chocolate sauce
garnished with candied angelica, and today on the stairs and in the
    elevator
the smell of mint chewing gum so that once again like the speech
bubble in a comic strip it's going to follow me all day.
Your lightdarkblue morning light, O city.
How many times have I thought to register this new color
with the International Lighting Association
as I was walking through the mud of busted arteries
and the coronary of transit, the smoke gushing out on the lines
and lights in the rush of pussies as hot as a scream
from a man hung up on the phone.
And the natter of car alarms, the racket of the convoy of cash
or the guy who has it, the whine of the ambulance, the procession—
everything that's still alive wants to live with a siren on.
But today I'm taking the park, I'm breathing gum, and the mud
smells of mint, and then the streets, the stores, the stands—
they've already dressed that mannequin, and still it smiles
at my wallet and my crotch, at my dreams, in which
I have a wallet, and I cross through the city
as the elevator of my saliva descends to the base of my esophagus,
like the glassed-in stairwell to the bottom of your dreams. In which
you have no wallet. You run through the streets all night,
sensational hi-fi is still blasting through the housing blocks,
and the city cowers, it pastes its glass buildings
onto the future, but it's getting bogged down, sinking, vanishing
into the mud, until someone spits his gum from the top

of a skyscraper, beneath the cloud canopy, and only a slight eddy disturbs the surfaces of the dustcloud. You tear yourself up with a scream and kneel at the foot of the bed.
Daybreak is breaking at your heels.

COLD RECEPTIONS

I.

In the end everyone chooses the summer sun
and not the cheery sleigh with the little bells.
Cold snaps will mess with our heads.
How long will we be in our prime?

To break our focus, to stream out
the small change of warmth—wouldn't our balance
be better were we to throw off these
beams of light? Or not throw

several dice at once, but hold on
to one and at most toss it
lightly in our hands? And maybe live
inside it, no longer to freeze

to the marrow, but shine with a tender
light that will also change
like my voice on the spectrogram,
right now? To perform this analysis

immediately. If only they'd want
to rub elbows in the white noise,
gulping us down, the snow.

II.

There are more strangers in this room.
The man who fell to earth and the last
man and the one who's best suit
was his first and last. Last! Last!
Why do they keep telling us our time is running out?
Our music does not recall their music.
Their games are rougher than our good times.
It'll get dark soon. Someone will raise a glass to the light,
measure a shard of glass among the ice cubes.
His wound is going blue like the crack in the glacier
I walk out through, behind my guide
into the due south of summer. Sleigh, sleigh,
the trees whisper in the gardens. The clouds
are still over the house, almost motionless.

LOVE AS A CATASTROPHE ON THE SOUTH SEAS

Good thing you found that black puddle by the forest,
there you have a basin of sky for beautiful ships
sailing the shadow line from eye to eye.
Your eyes will do. And if anyone says that, bent
over them with a smile fit for a king,
we are so poor, so what? We have nothing
but the sand hardening along the length of my ships
as they glide across the path, from sea to sea,
like *Discovery,* like *Adventure,* like that vessel of La Pérouse's,
your salty braids guarding the water's edge.

And the eczema on the sky's skin before twilight's assault
is so . . . gray, and that day, immemorial and heavy, like laundry
on the line—Come. I have something to show you. You'll see that sky
as it falls on the orchard, the twilight fizzing in the apple trees,
and like a golden beetle the moon wishes it could alight on your hair,
but first it needs to light up off the spark from the sun's horseshoe
as it jumps the water hazard. It gets me so very excited,
these pictures, archipelagos, Santa Cruz, the Sandwich Islands . . .
Who, after a fall, doesn't feel like a line gone dead,
as the sky keeps us waiting and waiting?
And those flashes in your pupils: is it my hair
spread out on the sand that's illumined them so from both sides,
or is it blood? Oh, if I were to visit those parts more often
I'd seek new passages, I'd dream of vacations in the country
and write of women who need not see things otherwise.

I'LL BE RIGHT BACK

These two women merged in sleep—
that's not how I wanted to put it.
At dawn a rain of hailstones, sudden silence.
I check a modest-sized bag. Here's the receipt.

We pleasure-cruise toward the mouth of the river.
There's a strange convocation on the lower deck.
I lean on the railing and admire the delta.
The magazine's next issue will be volcanic.

The doors open, there's some kind of mess hall.
The waft carries me north of the cash register.
Today, Ukrainian borscht and fillet of walleye.
The lone white sail of the fillet of walleye.

Someone leads me behind a monumental screen.
I think that we could do this *en masse*.
I measure a thin tie in the marketplace.
Someone sells me a ticket. I study the departures.

THE OCEANS

Quite delayed, I set sail on the great oceans
with the first auspicious wind. The beach is now sketched in the
     distance
by a line of breakers, in the cabin I'm brewing a mocha . . .
I set the yacht to drift . . . How I love these states
of inertia, as the boat dances like a leaf on gentle waves:
so great is this love that I'm overcome with torpor,
and first I scan the radio for some decent rock,
later I broadcast my thoughts casually into the unknown,
and on deck, napping away this entire tranquil day,
I reach into the boundlessness of things for what's yet unwritten,
thus to multiply our shared belongings.
But with the first word all thought is plunged into shadow.

How difficult it is, essentially, to understand this shadow,
which meanders behind me through all the oceans,
through the foam, like the *Flying Dutchman*, outpacing the day
on crescent-moon sails as it assaults the night with our belongings!
Torpedo boat of Evil! I wake up and pass quickly through all the
     states
of terror, fear, despair, like some drugged-out hero of rock
coming down from star to rock-bottom. Night has fallen. In the
     distance
the harbor lights, the lighthouse, nothing that I would call
     unknown.
I turn off the staticky radio. I hope the fragrant mocha
will help out, because something should be written
before the oceans play host to torpor
and I feel nothing but the dead swell of the waves.

I sit on deck and drink. By now I'm probably on a wave,
so I have to make sure not to go too deep into the shadow
of this cloud, which illuminates the moon and brings torpor
to my words, deceiving me with the thought that the only states
that fit are those approaching silence. The great masters of rock
are of a different mind, but when it comes to traversing oceans
I prefer silence, for I am only interested in what might emerge from
    the distance,
mute and unheard-of. In my mug the mocha
is swirling, the sails work lazily, and I'm checking what's written
already, bearing in mind that often it's only the dawn heralding day
that brings what the night has not, and that liquidates our
    belongings,
showering us with the glare of the unknown.

Such calm. On the horizon, a transatlantic liner sails into the
    unknown,
and perhaps I will yet feel the dying vibrations of its waves
or hear the music from its illuminated decks? They're dancing to
    rock,
the elegant ladies and gentlemen, oh, if only to fall into torpor,
for isn't that the aim of all our efforts? Only states
of euphoria and exhaustion, orgasm and other ecstasies, shorten
    the shadow
between what has been written and what remains unwritten.
And this is why we are enthralled by Him who arrives from the
    distance,
for He will inseminate time with light, and time will evaporate. My
    mocha
is getting cold. Friend, it is with a heavy heart that we leave our
    belongings
on shore before setting out on the vast oceans,
for there's no knowing whether we shall ever see so fine a day.

But for now the night promises that drift leads not unto day,
and that some star will lift us like a crane, suddenly, into the
    unknown.
Calm before the storm. What else could it mean, this torpor
of water and sky, what else but the threat that what remains
    unwritten
intoxicates me and draws me so avariciously to the oceans
that, wiping my green eyes on the merciless distance,
I'll say: Oh, it is not in a surge of thrilling rock
that I have found myself here, these are not the common states
accessible to anyone who indulges in such stimulants as mocha
or alcohol or narcotics, which turn a man into a shadow.
It is a matter of frequency, of the corresponding wave,
which you'll never catch if you're too concerned with name and
    belongings.

And then the wind said, "Go ahead, jettison your belongings—
just leave it to me, and you will see a day
that'll knock your socks off. Only, what's with the torpor
on the ship's side, the vacant stare into the sea's night, as if
    unwritten
were all you saw could ever be? What's with these melancholic
    states?
Take the helm and sheets, take me in your arms, because in the
    distance
adventure awaits. At first you can listen to some decent rock,
because music will help you sail more swiftly across the oceans,
especially that sort of light, aggressive music for which the shadow
of your thoughts simply does not exist. And then the unknown
itself will out, and in the blink of an eye of a wave
it will carry you off into cold inlets. And may the fresh mocha

scald your lips one last time, for later will be too late." The mocha!
Was the wind mocking me? The squall was so intense that all my
    belongings
started to knock around the cabin, and through the splash of waves
    I didn't hear the rock
that was supposed to have been the soundtrack to the start of my
    journey into the unknown.
I was picking up speed. The stars faded, the clouds like a great
    shadow
must have covered the whole sky, which, now black as the oceans,
trembled in the wind. Suddenly, a bolt of lightning lashed the
    horizon in the distance . . .
How can I know for sure that nothing has been written
there? That a quick *flores* of light in the sky or a zigzag on a wave
is not a sign meant to delight or press into torpor
those who, with such mixed feelings, are awaiting the day
of judgment? Though I no longer had time to plumb such states,

since I was listing hard into the pitch of darkness. The states
of the sea—that's what mattered. Of course, the mocha
had spilled, and what was left was cold. I swore that when day
came I'd make myself a new one, thus to overcome my morning
    torpor,
especially bad in light of my having spent the whole night on a wave,
during which there had been absolutely no chance of anything
    getting written.
Besides, it had gotten cool. A cold fog was covering the oceans,
or else my eyes, or my mind. Do you remember rock?
I asked quite loudly. Do you still cast a shadow?
Could you provide at least an approximate description of your
    belongings?
Isn't everything gradually immersed in the unknown,
doesn't it all lose its familiar contours in the uncanny distance?

Will you find something yet, something familiar in that distance,
something like bottom, top, surface, or depth? Are there certain
      states
that can be recognized, will there be just the swing on a wave
of inexpressible feelings and the boundless oceans,
which are an affront to all maps and names, such as Mocha,
Adélie Land, Warsaw? Will some cartography assimilate the
      unknown,
and in the roar of the waves and wind, like the negative of rock's
noise, in the wild tumult, will everything heave into the unwritten,
in an aura so strange that no one will know whether it's night or day,
here or there, what belongs to conscience and what is mere
      belongings,
because all words and syntaxes are leveled in shadow,
and reason will arrest what remains of torpor?

Oops, I've let go of the helm, and there's snow in my eye. Torpor
amputates all my members, the boat sails itself, and in the distance
white phantoms are looming. Is that the break of day?
And even if it is, so what? There's no longer any steam off the mocha
in the ruins of the icy cabin; the fingers strike no fire. The unknown
is already shining in the passes between mountains of ice, and the
      oceans
steam with a threatening light, like the stage at a rock
concert. Through frosted eyelids I see my boat speeding on an oily
      wave
into the bay before a great mountain . . . Has someone written
something there? No, I can't make it out. Perhaps a warning that
      such states
are an exceptional way of losing all of one's belongings
and making a shadow

of the man you once were? And still I see some shadow
on the mountain peak and here, through my torpor,
a whisper . . . as if of snow itself. Are these words as yet unknown,
can I expect to be mocked again by some false states
of consciousness, unconscious, since now they're dark as mocha
from the avalanche of signals from a frozen body rocked on a wave,
at the end of his rope? Will this dazzling day,
open above me like a parachute of snow, place what's been written
in parentheses and carry its own inscrutable content into the
        distance,
to place it in a tome whose covers run over with oceans?
Then nobody'd be able to say these were his belongings,
not even someone who, chillest in the world, listens to rock

on Cape Denison. Just as I am listening to rock
in my cozy room. You see! It's all just a shadow
of event and weather, a means of daily torpor,
sea-breeze out the window, hunger in the heart. A tasty mocha
is steaming in the kitchen, and through the shades the day
seeps in, and on another scale I now see our shared belongings
as I run, after a light breakfast, from wave to wave,
lodging to lodging, trying to find some unknown
medicine for such wounds as the hours inflict. These states,
these lodgings, who will take them in his arms? I know I'm in the
        distance
when, my heart trembling, I exceed what's already been written,
endeavoring to provide exemplary talk of oceans.

But aren't I like a shadow, if what has been written
barely brushes the unknown, just as each day
begins with a mocha in order to bring me to better states,
but then there's torpor and the sad torment of rock,
and I no longer know where the oceans are that, in the distance,
with each impact of the waves, scoff at our belongings?

FIVE FATHOMS DOWN

I

Imagine it is thus
A monotonous movement

Days sink in their standing
Hours die in their sleep

Mirrors approach through mist
And the watersong tarnishes

We speak through airlocks
Broken are bridges and rails

Broken

Our positions burned

2

In the evenings birds flitter in
Thin leaves of soot on the air
And it's the same in the blood's infrared
The same in night-vision
The head tossed back the mouth
Open for the shot
And ever the cricket's signal
To someone who must arrive any minute
Like the rasp of a drum with a broken snare

3

This will be one moment
And nothing will happen

And you're having fun up there
I'm driving the blood from my bright head

And when you descend deeper
I draw hearts on the mirror

I smile like a sandbar
At the ship on the surface

4

Clean yourself out
And lose your way

For the path is in losing
For the trace is in losing
For in losing us

A gray angel
And lightness beyond comprehension

So that what is dead will leave us
And something else cut us to the quick

This is how the dead fell from us
And left us no living thing

XVIII

But the receptionists don't have our reservation,
so they keep our IDs and bags at the exchange desk,
and we can freshen up a bit in the meantime.
I was beat. They'd wired the money to the chairman's
account, the board approved without a fuss, without even
putting it in writing, so what do you do? You didn't
want to go for it, and I was thinking: hold on, just a second,
are we talking wholesale or retail? Wholesale. Wholesale? Well,
gentlemen, shall I compare my red fingernails
to rays of winter sun? Am I to probe for some errant
bit of skin next to the goddamn fingernail of some bum
finger on one hand with the fingertips of the other and slowly,
painfully, pluck it out? The other went pale and said to the
    chairman: Yes,
but the two of you can go fuck yourselves, because I sent you
a fax of the original invoice, and what

came of it? Let's go over it one more time.
Generally speaking, I feel like Captain Kloss in the fourth episode,
when he lingered too long in the emptiness of the Turkish
bath, or else like a South African carrion plant,
which Poles cultivate as a decorative. And at the stadium
I run into a third guy: So that's how it is? You want
to leave it at that? But if you're afraid
I'll sink lower, I have a driftnet beneath me, and dreams
do with me as they will, as they do with you, so life
would be too hard if we were to understand one another,
because if we were to understand one another what good

would these dreams, or anything else, do? *They weren't holding.*
And that's that. The guy nestles his head into his shoulders
and flies like a pigeon, then he barely touches the ball
and scores. Try crooning to me.

Didn't count. And that noise? The second hands. Or the rush
of the spine in the ears. Let's spark it. And I hear: Where
do I know that face from? My name will tell you nothing,
for that catastrophe, too, goes as planned. But how many
of you are there? Old acquaintances? Silence. So I come
ashore and suddenly feel something like the cold glissando
of fingers on my eyes, like snowflakes, because there's one
in back, another, with a flashlight, in front, and two
on the sides lighting cigarettes. Brrr. And, anyway, Bernardo
and Francisco are dead, too, and so what? So I piss
all over everything and wonder to myself how, where, and when
to fuck off, but unenthusiastically, because they might be thinking
you'll die soon, and then they'll have their parable. (It's
funny that as you walk toward the exit you come on screen,
which is why it's so hard to see what's around you.) And just then
that priest shows up and says, *The oceans
will be discussed individually,* and I: Fine, there's no smoking
on the beach, glow with God, because I'm summoning snow
with both hands, though the future still enjoys
a certain fame among its own, but for me it's laryngitis,
occasional relations, vermin. To which he says: Huh? Wind
in the oculi and sand? And yet we have the voice and call

of God—hear how it runs by shortcuts, the way wind
levels woods, as you catch the bluish scent of lakes
and say "spring," "childhood," and drink more

tea. And that's your fate. When I sit like this and think
of how it's been four weeks since I've seen the sun—
tears. Did your father succumb, Copernicus? Oh yes, *he'll end you,*
so say the water plants and the water, which loves
the moon and flees so swiftly. Whereas I,
so that your tired little face might get some
rest (now the sheer shine is on the move, the leaves'
savage talons ascend even the stained glass of shadows), I could
simply take the moon away and do so much, so much! We still
haven't gotten my ethereal finish under control.

LOCAL TRAFFIC

That pain in the throat when the cold of a tear
tears the morning in the larynx like the lure
you were caught with, and now you must
dance on the line and find in that
dance a narrow space
and time: "payment of the fee

ensures a grave's existence for years
to come." For years? This so distant
relative of the man in question has lived
36 of them, and he's afraid of long walks,
the sun, bad nights, and the madness
of the day, but the rest is illegible,

the signature no exception, and it all
goes out like a thought striving
but unable to touch the acrobat's
dance on the wire. O beautiful years,
ages of ages, nights of nights and dials
of days on what was once an indispensable
necessity for merchants and bookkeepers!
When I blink my eyes like this, and that's all

I'm doing, just blinking, snapping
shots of mass-produced clouds,
while the eyes I haven't wiped,
like the spark from a Wimshurst machine,
chase after the rubber stamp in the hand
of the postal clerk—I'm drowsy
with fever, and my vertigo

is justified: What? So many
bills? Is there no one left
to buy us out, since there is no end
of decline, the zeroes multiply and gravity
drags the forehead to the windowpane?
Who's checking me? Where's the puck?
Nevermind, it's temporary. I've been
sick lately, and I've been riding the subway
like mercury in a thermometer
with an unfamiliar scale.

LOCAL TRAFFIC RULES

Nearly everyone pays exorbitant bills. One day I crossed the sandy road by the cemetery in Serock and was puzzled by the rules, "Rules of the Cemetery," a metal sign with a prominent header and a few barely legible words on a grey, rusty background. A drill, rules? A heat wave. I had just been sick for more than two weeks. Behind a stand of trees, on the banks of the Zegrze Reservoir, anglers were casting their hooks.

I was thinking not about Tadeusz Różewicz, but about bills and fees, in particular about the one the reticent sign was encouraging: ". . . payment of the fee ensures a grave's existence for years to come . . ." But I had the sun on the back of my neck the whole time, and I had to keep moving, from Serock to Jadwisin, not from Bordeaux to Nürtingen, but then I kept thinking of Hölderlin, of long treks, of the thirty-sixth year of my life. When did Susette Gontard die? It was then that, in a manner as mysterious as it was inevitable, Maurice Blanchot became entangled in my sentences.

I was struck by the notion that someone was dancing, but that someone else was benefiting rather substantially from that dance. For example, that people were "freeing themselves" sexually, but that at the same time an easy, erotic, calculated industry was blossoming, and production was up for books and newsletters that furnish sex with a permanent address. I have nothing against it in theory. The loss of truly free time and space is significant, but it is otherwise well established that nothing meaningful and free is ever registered as residing permanently at a given address.

Moving on, "what was once an indispensable necessity for merchants and bookkeepers" is an abacus. Some abaci were like drums, others like discs. Cf. Encyclopedia Britannica, under "abacus."

Of course, one could replace the verb "to buy out" with the verb "to redeem." Whereas, in this case, the placement of the word "left" signifies no hope of any kind. The bills are astronomical, the line presses forward, a man faints and suddenly hits his head against the windowpane at the postal counter; that somebody is like a stunned hockey player checked against the plexiglass.

But every day, even the worst day, in its infinitely subtle modulations, in the horribly legible turning of hours, minutes, and seconds, is like a sentence leaning slowly into the cool, capacious night of a poem. Only sometimes does it happen that the night is sleepless.

MORNING EDITION

Garrulous mornings, dynamic
departures from the take-off of night,
mouths filled with words that snap
like a parachute behind the fighter
pilot landing on an aircraft carrier. Stop,
I think you misheard that. I think
it's an Eastern European high pressure
area working on my nerves with signs
of sun beneath the still-closed
sluice of day, as the machinery
trembles before the grand opening
and the sun maneuvers toward the gates
already ready to enter, soar up, sail out
over the city with the dazzling pomp
of a heat wave. The rooks that spend
the night in the poplars in front of the house
have already flown to the fields,
but in sleep their dark racket was so very
talkative that I imagine it might be
possible to chat with birds
at some wild frequency,
head over heels, at daybreak,
because they run the same missions
at night as in the morning, so to hell
with the goggles and flight suit, let's
file classified reports on the position
of enemies and friends on the Ocean
of Storms and the Sea of Vapors, the Sea
of Dreams and Crises, on the Sea
of Tranquility. How did the moon

get in here? And enemies? Let's talk about
you instead: so what if you're lousy
on the jump? You glide right off
the edge, where there is no end,
and it's a long way down? Now
leapfrog: surely that umbrella
is a parachute? Sometimes
I'm afraid of this mumbling,
these words with missed connections,
from nowhere to nowhere, as if
my head shone ominously with lights
from a pinball machine, but under
whose control? Yours, or his there?
And do you remember Kloss? Ingolf
Mork! The inrun, take-off, flight
and landing: I go to the bathroom,
cold water, shower, splashes
of water like snow from under skis
and the head blown off the pint
into the faces of gawkers. I'd like
to jump that well, too. But something
doesn't want to pass my throat
after the landing: could it be
that the night is dumbstruck, dazed
within me, speechless? Let's
go get a beer.

POEM FOR J. S.

"Do your dance, Cooper."
—*Twin Peaks*

Friday, June 2: *Aktiv Vergesslichkeit* and *Gelassenheit.* Kuba and I
　　are going out for a beer, my head hurts
Something awful, and it's starting to drizzle: they say the heat
　　is ever mixing with the cold, the Eastern
European high with air of polar-sea provenance. Am I to be
　　humiliated? Will the pain and dizziness
Force me to abandon this poem here, now? We've had such volatile
　　weather of late, the day before yesterday
Light rain and golden luminousness on the street as I left
　　The Cock and then bam! gray globules of rain
From the cherry-gray sky, banners of watery dust on the roofs
　　and a rapidly growing grayness full of light
And water: birds soar to the leaves, people run into archways and then
　　the terrible clatter of hail in the heat! a flurry
Of leaves cast down through the air, a gust brings them to the arch
　　where I am standing, watching: this is Rakowiecka
Street, poplars, a great many teenagers taking the new subway line
　　to dance clubs and bars, oh, the fun
They're having: some of them throw up their arms and skip,
　　others run, babbling to high heaven,
While the shy guys wait beneath the awning of the empty vegetable
　　stand by the stop and deliberate. Hah! Lightning!
Thunder! The storm, back on the offensive. I wonder, how are the
　　rhododendrons
　　　　faring in the Academy of Sciences' botanical garden

In Powsin ("Some lovely new plants will be in flower by tomorrow,
        and really worth seeing.")? But I'm afraid
Of storms. That time in the country they made quite a fuss over storms,
    they pulled
            the furniture back from the walls, because lightning "runs"
Along walls when it strikes a house. But as a rule it didn't strike the house,
        though on the hill by the forest they showed me, um,
What were they? Belemnites or fulgurites? Then again, what was I doing
        in the country? As lonely as Krzysztof Karasek
With a beer by the kiosk? And then why was I hanging around Korea? I may
        have been happy. Strolling in a sweater in springtime
Or fall, it's such a delight in the garden: the quick chill of the hammock
        chord and the wind in the walnut tree overhead:
The book falls from my hands, and my nap teems with short-lived dreams
        with the gray-golden hue of rennet apples
And, Justyna, your eyes. This is all so unreal, I say to Kuba just then,
        one beer moves so smoothly to the next
That one feels the delightful tingling of time in the bones and wants
        to stretch out, not to sleep, to drink, smoke, soak up
The night, which breaks casually into being and then never breaks away
        from us, but clings like a moth
To the light: is this how we will be lead to our deaths? One more step
        toward the flame, don't be afraid, put out
Your finger, feel it, scream, laugh: it's merely a trifle, for this is neither
        the time nor the place for you to turn on your heels
And, laughing, to back away from the bonfire, into the darkness.
        My head hurts. We talk about the essay
Kuba is writing about B. Z., about the humble d-word
        that Bohdan will not call by name
Even though it's ubiquitous. The second beer becomes the third,
        and I warm to the idea that I won't work.
My head really hurts, and anyway even after just a little beer I am
        unlettered. So how will I finish my poem?

The tension builds. There should be a public outcry, "Get going, go
    home, pull yourself together!" but the prognosis
Looks bad, because when a few guys get up from the table in front
    of the bar just as we walk in, on a Friday
Evening at that, can you waste it? You could sell it. But how will I finish
    cleaning up? For your arrival? You can't
Just throw everything out: stocks of old drugs (Progesterone,
    50mg?), herbal Salvia Fix and 8
Septovit Fix, orange peels in some brackish marinade,
    Satural, two Pepto-Bismol bottles,
A couple dozen old pots, a blender, a meat-grinder (what's that rumbling
    in the garbage chute?), two rings
Of keys, seventy kinds of incredibly stale spice, some mittens,
    about a hundred plastic bottles from mineral
Water carbonated and still (a clatter as though the entire apartment
    building decided to go bowling
At the same time), strong aniseed candies, La Pasticca
    Del Re Sole, brought from Italy
In the late seventies, an old TV antenna that could do
    in a pinch for a hanger
But that mostly just threatened the beautiful eyes of inebriated
    guests, and that thirty-year-old fridge
That could freeze a two-liter bottle of Coke in under an hour
    and was basically impossible to adjust.
To be continued? For now I put on a pullover and think it should
    continue with the simple punch
That Tadeusz likes to call a "Charles Dickens": whiskey,
    hot tea, lemon. For the flu, nerves,
Podagra, especially for the latter, because for omagra there's only
    wine cooler made from Luksusowa vodka, fruit
Drink, and seltzer. (Whereas a *podgorzałka* is a duck, *Nyroca nyroca*.)
    But we're drinking beer, and it's getting

Dark: the temperature will go up and up until the quicksilver of laughter
    bursts the thermometer and the bar shoots into the night
Like a fantastic flare. Flares. My heart laid bare. Could it be that we
    had not a single fascination in common, sir,
My dear J. S.? Charles Baudelaire? And aren't I sometimes
    about the everyday, Tomek? I can be all
About the everyday and, almost like Jacek Podsiadło, I believe my eyes
    when Tadeusz and Justyna spring up
From behind, and now I'm ordering not two but four beers
    (Kuba takes care of the chairs). Oh, my head
Hurts the whole time: Justyna says it's from stress, Tadeusz
    suggests bison-grass vodka with apple juice.
Of course I'm nervous and tense, because tomorrow and tomorrow
    hardly bears the meaning Macbeth attributes to it.
I order a vodka and juice. An "Enter the Dragon." Tadeusz orders the
    same: tall
        glasses ringing with ice cubes: 100ml each, 100 years
Of health, Henryk, and who knows better than you how *that* passion
    relates
        to the grace of God? (That scene in Poznań:
On your knees, talking about Leopold Buczkowski, when into the hotel
    room
        bursts Janusz Rudnicki: what is it, Hen,
You performing a Eucharist?) What do you say to another? Fifteen
    minutes later I feel like the title of what may be Julian
Kornhauser's best book! And darkness has fallen in the meantime, it's
    gotten
        late, we're in a forest: a hundred people
Around us, high school students, college kids, ruffians, all so young and
    beautiful,
        so thick around the tables: a magnificent
Scene, this crowd in front of the Green Goose on nights in late spring,
    glasses in their hands all the way up to the edge

Of Independence Boulevard. Late-spring nights! At the edge of summer,
    when time is out of joint and the girls
From the "Bermuda Triangle" start to shift from one leg to the other and
    the neighbors
        from the tenth floor move out to the Mokotów Field
With a neck of pork, a grill, and 3 liters of spirit mixed with water
    and honey. On a night like this I went to Korea
With a bouquet of roses, so the schoolgirl would know her English teacher
    was ready for anything: these flowers,
As yet undelivered, but rather over the fence into a dark garden,
        were invoked in a little poem in the margin
Of a quiz. I got the address from the grade book. Did you take the song's
    moral
        (*Little China girl / you shouldn't mess with me*
I'll ruin everything you are) to heart way back then (1983),
        or was it a bit later? Shshshshshshshsh,
That was homework: *to mess with sb*: to have dealings with someone,
        but *mess* also means "havoc, chaos, confusion,"
And the rest should be obvious: since this was homework,
    I needed to have a home to finish it
Properly. And what else should one finish properly? One should drink
        the beer Tadeusz is bringing, God willing!
One should clean up! Clean up! Dig into the concrete of the apartment
        Like a beetle, the shady evil weevil,
The shoddy hatchback hunchback that lives on mildew, the museum
    death watch
        that destroys all the collections and archives (it even
Likes adhesive), like the dung beetle, the spotted spot-scrubber ant,
        the scabby scarab, *Brychius elevatus,* the hispine,
The ladybug and yellow-green and purple water beetles and that gorgeous
    clerid (*Thanasius formicarus*),
The white-red-black terminator of woodworms. Or your
        good neighbor, your strange neighbor:

This beetle, with a body length of approximately 8 to 12mm, has slightly truncated, tapered wing covers that diverge toward the sides. The female typically has black wing covers and feelers with short feathering on one side. The male, however, has orange or reddish-brown wing covers and feelers with long feathering on both sides. *Metoecus paradoxus* develops among ground-nesting wasps. Here one encounters a typical supertransformation (hypermetamorphosis). Toward the end of the year the females lay their eggs in a fissure in a dead tree, from which the wasps will collect wood to build their nests the following year. In early spring the larva hatches into its first larval stage, 0.5 to 0.7mm in length, the so-called "triungulinus." It has long legs equipped with hooks and is very lively. It waits inside the wood for the wasp, which carries it to its nest. There the triungulinus actively seeks out a wasp larva, penetrates it, and continues to develop as an internal parasite, growing very quickly. The wasp larva remains alive the entire time. Next the *M. paradoxus* larva eats away an opening in the trunk of the wasp grub and becomes an external parasite. It eats away another opening near the wasp grub's head and sucks out the contents of the grub's body. This is followed by a second molting, then a third shortly thereafter. In the meantime, the *M. paradoxus* larva devours the entire wasp grub, except for its hardened pincers. It undergoes its chrysalis stage enclosed in the cell whose lid the wasp grub had still managed to close. The adult insect emerges in summer and does not feed during its brief life.

And here we have a paradox, because from this standpoint none of us
        will ever graduate. "Shall I part my hair
Behind?" I think, meeting the gaze of one of my female students
        of English who a second later
Is lost in the dark throng of bodies as if in a thick forest. That's *selva oscura*,
        right? *Nel mezzo del cammin di nostra vita.*
(I'm no longer taking part in the conversation.) I'm so scared, James. "Why
        is this poem so long? And full of death?"

Your words. In July 1983 Piotr visited you, his first time
    in New York, oh, his first time past
Quarantine with a passport and a scholarship from the Department of State
    (the same one Bohdan had way back when?
His poem "The Day Stanisław Kania Stepped Down" gives the time
    accurately to the day.).
He flew in from Virginia to talk with Kenneth Koch and you
    and also with Edwin Denby *but*
He didn't reach Koch, and Denby said in such a gentle and polite voice
    on the telephone that unfortunately
He was just on his way to Maine. He wasn't on his way to Maine:
    he killed himself a few days later. "I know
What he was talking about," P. S. says on the corner of the miniscule
    garden of Brodzka Pub (formerly Gong). And
Schuyler? John Ashbery arranged for a two-hour sit-down,
    warning that Schuyler is difficult.
Hotel Chelsea. What floor? Second or fourth? "I was just
    dumbfounded by how poorly I knew him.
Sure, I had these questions, but such an unfledged shithead,
    on the one hand . . ." And on the other: J. S.
In a dark room, about 15m², as narrow as a sleeping compartment
    on a train, with dirty sheets, obese and unshaven
He just sort of . . . dragged himself up, put his legs down, and waited. "All
that
    together blew me away, but I had to
Keep up appearances, so I switch on my recorder and ask
    my questions, but that internal tension
Is always there and shows up so floridly in everything I say,
    and Schuyler says only, 'Yes, I think so,'
And 'No, I don't think so . . .'" "Well, it's great that you got
    anything at all," Ashbery said. "You know,
I later wondered what to do with it. I even thought it would be fun
    to publish the whole thing. And that's it:

That's the whole story of my unrequited love." Thank you so much,
    Piotr, because that's actually the whole
Story of *my* unrequited love. Pretty young ladies in Lucky
    Strike uniforms emerge
From the bustling dark: it's a special offer. You have to hide
    your Camels, Carmens, and Golden Americans
If you don't want to exchange them for Luckies or else just get four
    packs and a lighter for free. Or no, today
It's different: they're not giving out cigarettes, just some coupons
    and scraps of paper: what's this? They're already
At the next table, sometimes they vanish into the crowd and you see them
    again: are they coming to us? We'll know soon.
Whoever buys the most gets a bottle of Johnny Walker Red. Plus there's
    the lightning
    round for the best slogan, and for every 2 packs
You get a red token with a $-sign that you can exchange for beer
    at the bar. So many attractions! Would we like
To play? Oh my, we're already concentrating on the ads:
    we may be out of time already: they're so
Lame we might not even turn them in: "A Wave of Strikes" beneath
    an open pack of cigarettes?
"Strike Out with Us" beneath a lone cigarette leaning sloppily
    against the pack? "The Last Temptation of
Christ" beneath a pack with one solitary cigarette sticking out? Pathetic.
    I ask the lady who's leading
In the whiskey race, and by what score. 13? So I'll buy a carton and Justyna
    another, we have 20 packs and 10 beers, we're
In the lead. Oooops, time to buy more: a carton and then another carton,
    thank you very much and you're very welcome:
The situation churns like in a kaleidoscope. And we make eye contact
    with our most serious rival: I'm going
To my place upstairs for the rest of my money and those plastic bottles
    that survived the cleaning. Good thing

They have caps: I put them in the leather bag you gave me
for books: I run downstairs and off the bat buy
Hey! four cartons for one million two hundred thousand in the old
currency: the company girl gets flushed.
What's your team called? *Literature in the World,* I say, and she,
"I am sorry to inform you that 'Now
That's What I Call Poland' has moved back ahead of 'Polish Lit'."
"'In the World'! The magazine can't lose,"
I say, and I buy another two cartons. "Under no circumstances
can the magazine lose!" I slam my fist
On the table and buy another carton while Justyna stands
by the bar and gathers bottles of beer
And the terrifying gaze of the bartenders who have to pour it. Oh, so much
to tell! And what is potlatch? Potlatch
Is the national dish of Hungary. And what is the name of the canal
linking Biebrza and Czarna Hańcza?
The Suez Canal? My dear radio. With which words must I tell you
of the decisive moments at the watering hole
When the gawkers cheer and the captain of the other team and I
bid higher and higher, a pack at a time?
And I say (to my surprise): let's call it a draw. Because no one should
lose. And he, with pregnant words:
Indeed, let's call it a draw. Then a rain of applause and prizes:
baseball caps, cigarette lighters,
And a bottle of bourbon to share (worse?). And thus we drink
almost half a fifth of bourbon
And fall into a light melancholy (is it really so unusual
that I don't know how to imagine love
Without total devastation? After all, it would be a crazy fluke
if you were to succeed in leading it along a blind,
Safe course and stopping dead under a concrete roof with a mildly
sacramental inclination toward

Emotion, during which time essentially nothing is so mesmerizing
        as bridges burned. Therefore *Aktiv*
Vergesslichkeit? Abgeschiedenheit and *Gelassenheit,* my dear
        German meister? That's when Sean
Came with a truck to pick up those old blue armchairs
        and the gigantic television from Platts
Lane, when, before my flight to Poland, I'd just barely—alright
        already—managed to throw everything
Out into the mud of that cold April 1992, including my money
        and a black plastic bag stuffed with extremely
Esoteric notes for my dissertation: they're laughable, all these possessions,
        when you go out for your first walk
With the freedom of one who, looking back over his shoulder, sees
        London burning.). And what happens next?
Next we move slowly upstairs: Justyna, Tadeusz, Kuba, and I,
        with our cartons, bottles, and the gift canister
We received from the bar, and we sit down, unreal with happiness,
        in the apartment, I crank up the music,
We sit there smiling, Justyna goes out onto the balcony and sits
        on the concrete, leans her head against the bike
And has tears in her eyes. It's still night, and it starts to rain again,
        I stand in the middle of the room, I smile
At Justyna, at Tadeusz, at Kuba, Justyna comes back in and says
        something to the Dieffenbachia, Tadeusz
Picks up the phone and orders a taxi, and after about ten minutes
        I'm there by myself, I turn out the lights
And sit in the armchair: I sit there smiling in the dark, untidy
        apartment, lightly press the fingernails
Of my index fingers into the sides of my thumbs, oh, because
        it will be alright, because in a moment it will be
An overcast morning, and you will pass into the cold air over the Atlantic,
        because you've been in flight for two hours

Already, because you'll be in Paris before long, because soon you can forget
    those oceans, because a child was born
Under the volcano, because it will be a holiday and we'll eat cake, because
    in winter we'll go skiing, because someone has to
Save me, because we have ever fewer beautiful and difficult words before us,
    because you're almost here: come.

from
Convoy. Opera
(1999)

IN THE LABORATORY

How pissed we were at the cruelty of the laboratory.
The child's had another day's worth of regression.

Calm down. You just throw up your hands
whenever you see such a malicious waste
of material, especially of human material
of the highest quality, since we all know
that lack of replacement components can cause
a fiasco not only for our program,
but for all other programs that depend
on the head office keeping quiet. And all it takes
is one word for us to hightail it to the basement
for three hundred and seventy bottles
of the best champagne. But wait, no comprende—
all week no calls, no tip, no fax, not even
common gossip about learned heads
hung over the solemn circle of light
on the most serious table in this fucked-up
country. Sure, the chief's always standing by the window.
But these days he only looks out for a laugh.

And meanwhile this is where the future is literally
being made. The future! Which means: shorts, dresses,
muffs for the wearing, the shape of the lighter
you'll use to light your reeking cigar,
and even the taste of that cigar, even the very social
acceptability or unacceptability of a cigar
in public places and in general. Weather
forecasts. The shape of clouds. A policeman's humor.
All those goddamn remedies you take for the flu
and every step of the child now crying in its crib.

FROM COUNTRY AND COSMOS

No, the padre didn't see Legia's last match.
That night, from Tuesday to the championship Wednesday,
three masked bandits entered the presbytery
and stole the AV. But the only one they're looking for,

wonder of wonders, is the unusually hot-tempered friar
Dubas vel Tornado, who with a screech of tires
tore off in pursuit of the low-lifes
and is already in his third day of circling his beloved

country as if he's fallen into orbit. Yeah, and we're right
behind him with the siren on, without a chance, but with a camera.
They say that BP already has a pretty good description, but the TV
stations are all over themselves to get a shot of us with a cassock,

like a cloud of hail over Nowheresville, nowhere near
Humptown, which is near Radom, where Typhoon
drank his coffee and skimmed the paper. Jesus. A shame
you didn't see it, but by now he knows

the prick should have blown his whistle, and that the violent
protestations of captain and squad came
to nothing. These bums should have access
to instant replay, I'm always saying so, to resolve

such awful calls. And then it seemed that even the stars
were booing. Quietly, of course,
but continuously, enraged, constellations dressed to the nines
in the covered bleachers of heaven.

from
Zoom
(2000)

POEM FOR FRANÇOISE LACROIX

You're here, fleeting moment. And you, minor riddle.
I'd thought you'd been sent out on reconnaissance.
You could have been looking for more victims, more terrain.
You could have just whispered or called.

And you, sad eyes: are you seeing me off with your gaze?
Perhaps you don't want to say that there is nothing left
but seeing others to the door . . . with all the senses?
The half-conscious quintet expects divine compensation
for its journey, though squander is what they'd preferred.

As in a photograph: left hand
from another story, intriguing, imaginary,
as far as possible from a look of concern.
And yet this gaze contains such combinations
of sadness and concern, of logical resignation,
that one cannot write for long. Grief
is too simple. The riddle hits you in the face,
it opens the locks of your tears, because the soul is a soul,
it grieves, it's young, and finally it falls
behind us, like molted skin.
It has no place in the monstrosity of our now,
though nothing exists but the teratology of our now
(it's a melody, not a lullaby):
the fairy-tale fender-bender & scrap heap of past & future.

Everything ultimately comes down to harbingers.
The adversary is condescendingly genteel.
With the hum of the escalator escalating
the halftones of wrinkled leaves, like globules of green water

on pitch, on their crazy side, without margins,
through the locks and into the wide, basically cold, world.
Wind. Still in my armchair, I rise above the floor:
my chair extends its bilateral wings.
We fly over the balcony's balustrade,
we turn above the poplars and toward the sea.

And at the seashore the wind must howl and waves roll
loud enough not to hold on to life.
Only to sleep like a stone at the end of a private beach.
After 7PM the ferries run one after another.
The rumble of long-distance engines dies away within us,
the lights go on, nightclubs sailing northward.
A tempest tomorrow. The fleet will go to sea.
It will stop, duly chastened, when it hits the wind.

MINOR DEGUSTATIONS

Where will our match be, the guys joked,
when will it be our turn to run onto the turf, inspired,
Salicional, Flauto, Gamba, Vox Coelestis bringing up
the rear, so dainty, so infallible from a distance?
But that's Barcelona—don't you remember that attack?
You will exit through the stained glass, hopefully with Miss X.

And then the fog was as solid as a ceiling,
though the forecast was for morning mist,
polar clearings and slight accumulations
of lacy dissonances and tears. Fine.
We tobogganed down the cathedral roof,
a nice gothic, a first-rate crust of snow,
and the brilliance of distant bells like a parachute.

But inside, a sympathetic priest was celebrating
a popular edition of our immortals.
But how about a swig? Perhaps some carbonated hemlock?
Meanwhile, the cigarettes were weaker and weaker,
and we pretty much started to lose our breath.
Only degustations, no decent consumption.
And unhappy visitations of the end of this sale,
though the actor and publisher are now certainly at "home."

And what good will it do? What good?
When our friend the switchman arrives,
when he orders us to dance the sardana
like genuine catatonics? I allowed myself

to mix a bit of wine with orangina
and feel a bit nauseous after that "stained glass."
The pleasure will not be mine.
The pleasure will not be mine.

MINOR DEVASTATIONS

Everyone is on the lookout for minor devastations
in themselves and in others. And throughout the world.
And it's nobody's fault. Angelic gehennas,
genes, as in genesis. Lawsonia and henna.

A voice bristles in the throat. Essentially the dark sky
and neon threads of mycelium in the enchanting forest,
as if that voice were always before you, twisted
the caps off mushrooms like light bulbs, and wiped out the lamps,
installing unadulterated darkness all around, shady flickers,
a faint undergrowth, a discreet swirling under one's feet
like the ground's very own diplomatic excuse,
a whisper, a wink of sand in the eye of a well.
When the forest set slides beneath the stage
and a new audience quakes with laughter
like the sky in a drizzle of falling stars,
there will be a change of scene in my vision,

it's warm, hot, boiling, scorching, scalding, and it's

here. Someone's stuck his hand in. It ate it up.
Then he ran as if burned and kept trying
to tear the air, for in the end it all
slipped out from under him,
drawn away on a short chord,
taken down.

TE QUEREMOS

The glare is radiating off us as we seize the platform
with our silly italics, lugging dead weight,
lugging our crap with a shirt, with cologne,
onto the transport, and the lady at the snack bar
will give us a plate for our ash-pack,
and the smoke doesn't bother her, nor do
our live bugle call and other popular hits,
she just asks for a smile in the ancient juvenilia
that disappeared somewhere in the athletes' village.
Someone was sentimental and spoke till exactly
a quarter past metaphor, then you can go,
a quarter of an hour till the train, time for us to fly
in our own obscure directions: we love this glare
from the Luftwaffe, they're so clean, so clever, however,
like one who squeezes someone's hand in the frenzy
of light in the October leaves, when it's
the world that falls to pieces, the eyes are dazzled.

[And one fine day after years of detours . . .]

And one fine day after years of detours we finally
arrive at the border crossing in our trucks at the appointed
place in the parking lot where there's a little bar called Zoom
and how nice it is to stretch, wipe our hands clean of sweat and
    grease
after years of bumming around downtown and at night on
    communal paths
our children are falling into each other's arms, but we're strolling
    along
conjuring up what books we've located in town.
And it's such fun in the parking lot when it appears
that Piotr is already halfway through one of his, God
he's fast! The waitress is kind enough to put some tables together,
but there's such a ruckus on the upper level,
so we go downstairs to be alone.
Our hello how are you kisses were like dying stars,
someone was watching us from the other side of wet binoculars.
The women are pouring out the contents of beautiful new
    handbags,
laughing over all their ill-got gains.
We explain to the children the last words
of the language of the country we're supposed to be headed to.
Our long road rambles within us.
We'll sit here "till it hurts."

from

Taxi

(2003)

LOVE PARADE

And were it impossible to show yourself from . . .

any side? Such a beautiful don't bother,
the devaluation of light, mirrors, shots, time
fucked over, pregnant with TV spots. Mr. Mole,

my friends. Even he has a dynamic side
that demonizes his frienemies. Unfortunately.
Sticking with the mole, and not just with the mole

in spirit, with a dispirited body, a warm, nasty body,
sucking oxygen and constantly bulldozing, acing
the serves, rushes, ping-pong balls of air, negotiating

points of apathy, velvet, and that one
and only off-limits and extraterritorial
corridor, easily, subversively calling off

we do this, we do that, Mole, when a mole is naked and not listening,
two of those solid sopranos, poorly configured? A shame,
kaput, "lost that loving feeling" at banquets and on bridges, for

whatever he writes, so much for life?
And who's telling us this? Who's crying so?
Madame du Deffand? Madame de Lespinasse?

POEM FOR THE READER

A misty lake. On the road to the bay
we had rain in our faces and wild strawberries in our mouths.
Didn't feel like wiping clean. Torrential horizons.
Evening came, tearing off the black tarpaulin.

In time, the moon. Next to the skeletons of fish,
i.e., a cloud, but as radiant as a crocheted lampshade.
And then the arcosolium in the wall of the forest bunker
to which our trench of wild strawberries led . . .
no, that's too lovely. Staged
in Chinese penumbras, just for you.
Don't bite your lip. Now you have blood on your mouth.
From those wild strawberries. Let's go, there's nothing here.

My dear twilight. What was there supposed to be, why this
    nothing?
I remember the rain of barcodes in your eyes
when I turned you into a moth. Fare thee well.
Like a bow made of smoke, you bind my flashlight's beam,
you flutter like mad and fall into my hair.
In my hair there is no refuge for moths,
Moth, my hair is hell, unsafe haven,
black snare, Medusa, dew of our blackest depths.
Now look. Those are Ivans. Have the last word.

OTHERWISE

The train is swimming with tones, concentrated signals
on the outskirts of momentum—as if movement
suddenly constituted a territory with fluid borders,
a pulsating contour let loose on the rails,
a cloud of steel, of flashes, rasps, and rocking,
a plasma of warmth trembling like a jellyfish-shaped stain.
A fish-bellied stain? I'm afraid you're overdrawn, sir,
you'll have to leave the warehouse. Heart, I'm sorry,

some other time, after the pointless inspiration passes.
We have to stop for now, because we have a connection.
Valdi? Which moods dominate the post-environmental
sections of Desperados and Yassasineros?
Is none other than Miss Heliotrope our bed-guest today?
Will Miss H. respond to the questions of the Kiddisons,
the Intrusivetons, as we might say, straight from the saddle?

The sun. You're so fond of meanings, sir, but you can't get them
without a reserved seat in the so-called narrow compartment.
You return needlessly to that stuffy compartment, though you could
just as well stand in the corridor and open the window,
stick your head out, follow the sparks of your ardor with your gaze
as they drift away, for jostling about, sending signals, slinking
    away—

it's for mere mortals, as may have once been written
by a German poet? We're not a German poet.
"Wild Thing," the train blares. "Gloria," the ties broadcast.
(A grocery car like a triumphal arch;
I'll take the bottom shelf, between the beverages.)

A LESSON IN LIVING LANGUAGE

And when someone dies, we say that his life
is now at the top of a great waterfall.
Then the liquid gods burst into a laughter
you can hear for many, even very many happy returns.
For some reason we call this laughter "the spider's kiss."
Anyway, it should be "feet" instead of "returns."

And there's no path here, thicket and Windy Bows,
a confusing terrain, then just wilderness,
though there's a lake, Wiatrołuża, and beaver lodges.
"Lodges!" we scream, and run into the ravine.

And here's another, Kamionka, where you could drown.
And which is also a river; a river is joy to the beholder.

Or else I run the board with my head held high.
Until a flying saucer suddenly sucks me up to the ceiling
like a ping-pong ball at a lotto drawing.
Or: maybe No One crossed it off. The jackpot's *grande*.

We also say "he passed," "he departed quickly."
We'd rather say, *Ziiuu iiuu*. Or *Ziuu aauu*.
My people are ready. They've started to walk the earth.
When they curse, all they say is: Kurt Schwitters! What a shame.

MY PEOPLE

My people are awkward, devoted to themselves
and to the remote expressions of the unreliable joys
they keep on the tip of the tongue as a "faithful" talisman.
It phosphoresces and illuminates the sadder fragments.
What am I saying—
                            the whole. At some remove my people
harden a bit, but in the motionlessness of my people
you can see departure—the hands splayed
at hip-level, drawn an appropriate distance
from the hips, the palms turned
downward. In essence settled down,
in short winged, the runaways, scarcely proficient,
in secret, in fast vehicles, in all
directions, run all over the tracks to retract
the horizon's signature.
                            Woe to thee. But do we
have veto power? Little bells, lamps, stoplights, the network
singing at the switch points? Indeed we do.
Like the strum of a fretless string, but it's . . .
fine. Some other time. Perhaps some other time.

THRAKT

The man who went away
is not the man on his way to us now. The day
closes on him without undue glory, the day
of another man, now gone. Sleep
sends him a sheaf of shadow through the keyhole,
but the buoyant draft
is dead on the threshold. The veranda
smells of apple, tea, angel food,
the dead sea of the autumn sun, because
the one who went away was only here in summer,
the one who's coming won't be here before winter comes.
But the scratch of the key goes on for months, is
like a corridor for sleep. Like thinking of another
road, as happens in the half-whisper of spring, when
the ancient wind reaches us from the river. Then
the key will be lost in the course of a night crossing.
Each time will be a hasty mess.

So homogenous in autumn gold. As sheer
as the celadon wave that came to a stop,
overhanging the little house by the woods. But the absent
shed tears at work, in town, among the cafés
where the good life is lived. Time
for *ballades et rondeaux.*
For—by the pontiff's good grace—heterodoxies
over cups of coffee, with liqueurs:—this is
undoubtedly how it should be! So long as
the city, the poor infrastructure, chews them up like a mill,
people will die along their route, without the halo of *symposion*

in trumped-up time. Oh, so there are no limits?
They've been canceled in clubs and neon? There is
decidedly less and less jazz. The dancehalls are quarries.
With colossal desire to profit not far from the healthy path,
man works it. It's a long time
since time set out on galleys, finding ports in galaxies
of stars that were the only thing that had made it happy. Though
such an image, such a likeness, was more than it could manage.

Is there a substitute *en masse*? Nothing of the kind.
All the jewels in the world won't enclose divine Astraea
in watches. Only the little corners of the seconds
of Southern music's deep silence are beautiful. The one
who's coming, however, dreams of a bed in a keyhole, of a tight
chamber most thoroughly in contact with the eye and with time's
brief tear. And that's what I want, too. Sleep
then breathes the river's flow, the wind
of the free motion of what is, in a divine sense, true.
But we are, understandably, dipping
out of phase, and everything is happening as if behind our backs,
even the really awful stuff, so there's no need to pretend
that we'll grasp any of this. And that's essentially
all there is to it.

O white veranda by the woods, TV room in the abyss,
where we've enjoyed so many pleasant evenings,
negotiating a round and a ritual cigarette before sleep.
Not a word of tears, though I felt time on my wrists
like sand and maiden's hair. Like shooting down
a tall slide into a night full of time and ignoring the pool,
where there might even have been a silver marsh of razors,
of retired sailor-girls. Thus the need to reinsure

the sirens, even in a wreck so illuminated by terrible silence.
It's hard to be a good comet after the fact. That's right. A late idea
doesn't hold the element that burns so intangibly
in the trembling hinterland of the stars. Divine mockery,
while we're on the subject, this experiment with memory, and a
　　　travesty.
That is, with such time as never was, and which you don't have,
because the only happiness is the time when time seizes you
once and could just as well keep you or throw you away.
And just like that every young person tries to be thrown
in order to be able to live, only now without happiness,
without time, in climates that are nondescript all of the time.
　　　Beyond
happiness, we are at best concerned with art.

Seeing the world off in this way, listening to sitcomical cries
and looking back on squandered bridges, getting bogged down
in the dispirited hours and, with each passing moment, farther away
from whatever the moment could possibly be—this is the divine
paradox and hat trick. Seeing the world off
on a train? From the very beginning
with a growing deck: of handkerchiefs, or kisses? To the station,
as usual, at dawn. Who
says to whom: I sort of fell in love? *Jehanne de France*?

And just as happiness is most intangibly the non-divine state
of the *imaginable,* in which God has furnished his antidote,
irony aptly instantiates the heart as the great mystery
of non-belief, or the hunger for infinite happiness possible
solely in time, and in time singing with the greatest affection.
Hallelujah. Have they already announced it on the megaphone? Rare

is the youth today who leans over a rose; he has no need of a
    superlogo
for existence. A Leyden jar is rocket science, as far as they're
    concerned,
and these are the sorts of things I've explained most insistently.
The express train *X Is Falling Down* is running late, etc.
You're lying on the platform, raised like a veranda over an empty
    field.

POEM (TRACKLESS)

The poem loses its memory around the corner
In the black air you can hear the guards calling
I was looking for my sister and couldn't find her
I had no sister and thus could not look for her

I had no sister how can one use memory to reach
Back along a street long gone
In our neighborhood lost in the courtyards
It doesn't know bright and early It's drinking in basements

Dreaming the hours away by the dumpster wall
My dark eyelids are heavy with wine
The poem leaves home and never comes back
The poem does not remember the home it never had

For this dark love for an uncivilized genre
Back along a street long gone
It walks without memory and vanishes without trace
There is no poem memory sister no home

TRACKLESS

And who is it who makes
the battalions, paratroopers, and armored divisions
so beautifully that in the salon of the *Decameron*—is that it?—
pretty much everyone swoons and begs for more?
An oxymoron? No need for us to be awed,
we have to whisper sweet nothings, listen gratefully,
and the telling will turn into beauty, my girl.

And each in his own time takes his position at headquarters,
and each starts out composing a few melodies for the ballet
of submarine dancers. And my siren?
Some strange fruitfulness stole away into your blouse
after its last cleaning—tell me what that is. Oh,
I cross my heart. Oh, I won't guess—Theophan-theomatic?
The moon like a cold shower after the sun has set.
Dark dawn for breakfast, with the end of the story.

Waking up in the sand is for the movies.
But one would still have to bless the sky
from a bird's-eye view. Into rain, paratroopers, reverse,
lyrical in the likeness of Westerplatte,
the flight of little drops, the rainbow, the sun's smile
as they take their own path down in fours to the beach,
all together. Would this have something to do with Jamaica
as Hel? I crawl forward on all fours, I walk out and come back
unconscious in Jastarnia, I wake up in Jurata,
conscious and redeemed, on vacation—

                                    this part
wasn't in the movie, which cannot be cut short
once it's been cut. Once it's been started.

FROM THE LIFE AND TIMES OF A LITTLE DOG

into mountains or sea or sky, leaving
behind: me, wag.
—*John Berryman*

Evening, the street you're walking is still quite blue,
unclear whether you're walking the dog or the dog you,
calling "come on," and the mutt overcomes its own sloth,
a geyser of dirt like the flim-flam of moths
and the dog's long gone toward the end of the street.
Stay cool. The customs agents, rich in their expertise,
each having let a carload of coke slip out from under his nose,
are humming: Speedy Gonzales. What, have the roads
of boring Warsaw, here, in Mokotów, struck
this little dog dumb? And what kind of talk
is this nosewriting, discourse into the blue afar,
the tiresome faraway of a district no car
could traverse or reach, as far as the eye sees
(a shame to start the race, pursuit of plebes
 in the eyes of residents who, as if on the mark,
stand in their windows and watch)? You have a smoke
(cinematographically), silence, emptiness, chill,
it seems there's nothing the matter, and still,
where are you going, hitting your heels
after the irretrievable runaway dog of the real?
Your inner voice says: he may as well disappear.
You can nothing your beast in the hundredfold gears
of esoteric knowledge, always caught in its traps,
even in a poem that refuses collapse,

for the symbolic dog was made to destroy—
"symbolic," yes, but also an axiological toy.
Un chat supérieur, writes Maurice Blanchot.
This sounds like a challenge, so you stamp out your Marlboro
and move like percussion, with a Nosferatu's rage,
warning the consequences that you'll clear their stage.
Your outer voice says: watch out for the lights.
O lights! Leave your worry to delirious tikes.
Doggy! Are you after a cat that jumps like MTV?
I hear a sensuous text, like from Motor City's
stables, I'm setting the mood with this wild noise—
the waitress who, her tray full of beer, flies
into the mix, and into a pole, her legs also flew,
as graceful as origami colliding with brew—
this is the quiet ambience to my steps as I fly,
shaking the foundations. In my over-sharp eye
I've now had a glimpse of the prospects to tap,
things looking so-so. A virtual blasting cap
starts to blow up our winter supplies
in the Sensodyne regions and behind the eyes.
Call the police. As Idea. The lines now cut,
along with the houses, *zusammen,* the street
falls to ruin, like wasted lances the ranks
are sleeping beside villas, headquarters, banks—
I've now hurled past three streets and more,
a mad accordion of overhanging floors,
till bubbling neon crowns me with its ghostly flow . . .
Babylon has fallen. We will never know
the story of this bog, nor of any Sweeney
to feed the fantasies of some future Heaney.
The glasses shattered, poochie. Now the score,
of course for tonsure, bass, and petit four,

exclusive and right-on, Czech for *let's go,*
as said by Zbigniew Machej, scribe *comme il faut.*
But moving on. I'm thinking, Old Yeller.
Dithyrambic canine, did some feller
light your fuse, make you rush "into the unknown,"
while I, close-reading your trail, choke down
cholesterol in a heart that does not beat for this?
We are enchanted, like a Prague *divadlo* dismissed
to Tanganyika or Éjur. I pray for chances
to restore the ranking and reclaim the nuances
of stores of eschatology, that you'll get yours . . .
that you'll break even!—my memory's scrolls
are falling apart, and I get lost in gaffes,
running into the field by Kabaty's gas
station, where the dog elegantly lolls
by the woods, a dashing smile above the balls
of the metonymic bone he's pulled from the earth.
"You think that you've lost the dog of the Sublime,
let loose in this vortex of deceptive mirth?
Too bad. Cyprian Norwid, in his 'Me Nego' rhyme,
descended no deeper into the discourse of shades
than thee—in the interest of deconstruction!
According to my program the comics are made
the opposite way. Observe the bone *sans* restitution
of letter/spirit play: skeleton, scaffold, a Czech
Republic of meanings, Hollywood lit with halogen.
Return to town, take a whiff of the wreck.
Revive the waitress, and try to save the beer,
go be a Modernist, perform the rites,
for laughs, of *stil nuovo,* make the links appear
a little differently: Dante's great technique
inflected with Lego's line of Technics,

and Microsoft has fallen—so the choir sings.
Tomorrow we'll create lives as amazing
as Sunday, as Queneau would have, clone the avant-garde
with the Cheshire Cat's smile taking the rear guard . . ."
And style the cat's smile? Puppy, we'll go through
all of this at home; for now it's time to bid adieu.
The dog and I will stare silently into the sky.
The sky suggests we have some eau de vie.

RETURN OF THE LITTLE MATCH GIRL

The Little Match Girl sets out on a long journey
by plane, only then they confiscate her matches.
It's a non-smoking flight. Now what will become of her?
A Little Girl, you see, only no Match,
much as the Match remains itself without the Little Girl.
But here I foresee horrible catastrophes, something

right out of Trakl. The eponymous lady-friend
trimmed down, without qualities that will beautifully
consume themselves in the fire of another story . . . and then what?
                                                              In the ether
all news has the same fundamentally heartening effects
of giving us more or less the same split-second reaction time.
The title comes off the marquis, the marquis off the façade.
The ether plays Marienbads with itself.

Marienbads are something Tadeusz can explain.
I, however, wanted to speak on an entirely separate matter.
                                                        Namely,
I can still remember my dream in which there were pears
or playthings by a cold lake, as well as wild roses
and swans—in essence, the kind of lovely supply compulsory
for fall, for this was naturally a poetic dream. So now,
Weh mir. Subsequent images were out of left field and shattered.
You can have the ball, there, under the pile of glass, like snow.

MUSIC BOXES AND MARIENBADS

"Music boxes!" we shouted, running with our bags down Marszał-kowska in the afternoon. "Marienbads!" Sheets of glass reached us, windows falling from the upper floors; I thrashed around like the moon on ice cubes. Then, suddenly, a chain of arms plucked me up, and I was rocking above the crowd, to vanish like an anchor in a dark hold. I'd been taken aboard.

Now I have the vague feeling of being on the water. The light fades rhythmically. Is it nighttime already? Is someone playing *Gaslight*? The fasteners of my nerves shine like clips on a torn sail—in the sun, which looks so decadent in this insatiable disaster! Time? It is! There are—dark days, like a smear of blood on a slide under the pressure of an ill-meaning lens.

"So then you are of the opinion that a stone can bleed."

"Of course. It's the play of sunlight on the domino's aventurine."

"Alright, heart. Six or seven words. *The poor benefit of a bewitched moment? The poor benefit of a bewildered moment?*"

"Quoting. The point is the play of *benefit, bewitched, bewildered, a, the, poor.* Domino. A domain oddly swept, that without hissing, wept."

(We can hear a foghorn blaring in the distance.)

We burst into laughter for the ages. It nevertheless brings us to tears when we note the Elizabethan corpse in the breakneck musical turns, as we register the observed lightness and sense that a gap is opening overhead, thin as mica, a glittering, sunny sheet. We hear the applause, but all this applause is a parade of tears on a watch crystal. O High Chamber! Like escargot, I come out on the wet deck, in stone silence, too half-dream explosions and cheerful salvos: hey there, slivers of isinglass, solid hematites.

To be wildered, to be witched, music boxes.

Bewildered and bewitched, Marienbads.

EMERGENCY EXIT

You say that life abandons us so completely,
turning us into experts and authors of life. Which means,
something for something. Your CV is taking on color,
you're sure to fulfill yourself completely, everywhere.
We will read you. Dying with laughter?
Weeping bitter tears over your presentation
to advance the investigation. Is there something I should know?
A length of string, no ball. A ball, no string
in reach, in sight. In a distant land
we gave you the slipper of good fortune. A diamond clog.
Now go sing to yourself as you please, because the shakes
are the shakes, they say, and they're right. The ball, a farce
of string, enchanted lights on a linden in an enchanted wood,
flask under a bench, pipe, pickle?
Touching measures. A dark game over the fence.
Chewing the buffalo grass from the bottle, waiting for the cows
to come home, as the detective waits for the spine to tingle
with better news, complaining of "the temperature of life"
while he holds the vial of laudanum to the light that retreats
in the pipework, in the weightlessness of violins.

from
Where the End of the Rainbow Doesn't Touch the Ground
(2005)

THE SPEED OF LIFE

What? I'm fine. I'm falling asleep.
Window, bed, dark. The chills
are the minimal sensation under the blanket,
the head stuffed into dreams. Dreams
are supposed to be like sand,
and are. Behind the lips. On the lips, grit,
glue, cobweb, and laughter,
glue, cobweb, and grit. G, c, g,
gggggggggggggggggggggggggggggggggggggggg!
A fatal error has occurred. Okay, but they
don't write it in Polish. It's fine. *Straszliwy
błąd miał tu miejsce.* Occurred, took place,
assumed its position. Over the covers? With a pro-
position. With an uncovered post-

position.

"A NEW CAREER IN A NEW TOWN"

The death of the author greets the promotion of his new book
(though nothing changes the fact he isn't with us).
His spirit is with us, just like the graviton, coronium.
His spirit lives among us.
  It appears that they already have the first email address
  for the moon, a promotional address for all: moon@moon.xnet.
  You can send a message, starting today.
  Astronauts will check the messages in a few years.
The death of the author greets the promotion of his new book
(though nothing changes the fact he isn't with us).
His spirit is with us, just like the graviton, coronium.
His spirit lives among us.
  It appears that they already have the first email address
  for the moon, a promotional address for all: moon@moon.xnet.
  You can send a message, starting today.
  Astronauts will check the messages in a few years.

from
Post-Rainbow
(2007)

from POST-RAINBOW

[it does not do to do but in the bathtub . . .]

it does not do to do but in the bathtub
or in the shower or only in a hotel
in a glass stall with a bright dome of water
(the glass granite dark tempered)
chatting only with the rustle of warm water
and ever so grateful that so warmly
dreamt of spring once summer once fall
writing on the water only seasons and castles
[*not for you to read*] last of the drivel
or in the fresh air in lovely country
maybe in a wood by a river or at a gas
station in Szeligi or near Mount Giewont
dreamt of winter ran in a line one doesn't
dream of winter I stopped running

•

[And so the days flew by and nothing really happened . . .]

And so the days flew by and nothing really happened.

Fine.
    And at the same time less and less solmization
on the air, it's really getting uncomfortable and interesting,
it's getting cold, chimerical, pharmacological.
Today (it's November) we have a day like any other,
we go to a restaurant and only order brandy and dessert,
we're warmed by *flammende* at the table by the river—
      strike of matches, flick of lighters,
      not a glass in the house that's not on fire.

And sitting by the river yesterday we saw a whirlpool.
It was a steady, apparently stationary whirlpool
that appeared to be falling in love with us.
It would draw something in and suck it down,
wink like an eye of alarm, icon of the storm.
Tremble of pipes in a faraway system,
for all of a sudden a distinct *pop!* and I had the impression
we're descending straight to your desktop and
                    ha ha
little lyric. We drink time's brandy. As long as there's
a whirlpool, we drink. Wir trinken und trinken
brände der Zeit, Brandy der Zeit.

•

[In daily life we rarely say a word . . .] (1)

In daily life we rarely say a word that might otherwise serve a national poet in the throes of inspiration. We won't say polka, but— dance—"taniec." Jaka jest krótka treść tego wiersza?—"What is the basic content of this poem?" Ton robi muzykę—"The tone makes the music."

In life, then, it's all about how something happens: jak, w jaki sposób—"how, in what manner." "Everything is passed from hand to hand"—Wszystko przechodzi z rąk do rąk. The merchant gives "the buyer"—kupującemu—"the goods"—towar. The buyer gives the "seller"—sprzedającemu—"money"—pieniądze. And so on, round and round: someone gives something to somebody else. Listonosz daje panu [jeden] list—"The mailman gives the gentleman a letter."

•

[Love like a raspberry patch with vodka . . .]

Love like a raspberry patch with vodka on a block of ice
with a gray undergrowth of pepper and a blush of Tabasco. They say

"shirt of flame" for the monastery's shot of mad dog. They say
milk and honey on your chin, Joanna.
They say

"tremble of pipes in a faraway system,"
"lallen" and lallen; "bittersweet"; *zuzu*.

They also say amazing dope, neanthezine.
They say alpha-O-mega or ode-e:

Apollo, the Lute Player, Ziggy Played Guitar
(some ways ash, some ways funky).

So let's maybe go to Poland Springs—

Tadeusz knows some restaurant

•

[In daily life we rarely say a word . . .] (2)

In daily life we rarely say a word that might otherwise serve a national poet in the throes of inspiration. We won't say polka, but—dance—"taniec." Jaka jest krótka treść tego wiersza?—"What is the basic content of this poem?" Ton robi muzykę—"The tone makes the music."

In life, then, it's all about how something happens: jak, w jaki sposób—"how, in what manner." "Everything is passed from hand to hand"—Wszystko przechodzi z rąk do rąk. The merchant gives "the buyer"—kupującemu—"the goods"—towar. The buyer gives the "seller"—sprzedającemu—"money"—pieniądze. We give "our relatives"—naszym krewnym—and "acquaintances"—znajomym—gifts—"podarunki." And so on, round and round: someone gives something to somebody else. Listonosz daje panu [jeden] list—"The mailman gives the gentleman a letter."

•

[See, Images! I'm your Touchstone Pictures . . .]

See, Images! I'm your Touchstone Pictures.
I'm your Twenty-First Century Boy & Fox.

A virgin is dozing over a crime thriller.
Her dream, like a moth around nightlights,
likes the emoticons of stars in the still sky.
She'd love to meet a man with a car that won't stall.
She'd meet to love a man at the casting call.

We visited the sky the moment things got started.
Time in retreat, Little Princess, and at the same time
the swirl of galaxies, waves, frequencies. The "glosses"
(*whisper:* for how many voices!) penetrate the ether,

a pure space opens up like a letterless
bottle in the surge of spheres, its vacuum
in ascendance. Though the resonance, the echo: whether
it's *echt* time (lesser) or it's not *echt* time,

when it happens, fall comes and happens,
a shadow comes over the pregnant beach, albeit
not the way an angel does ("stranger than angels,"
Archangelsk), from trope to trope, hop-hop.

A virgin is dozing over a crime thriller.
Her dream, like a moth around nightlights,
likes the emoticons of stars in the still sky.
She'd love to meet a man with a car that won't stall.
She'd meet to love a man at the casting call.

•

[I eagerly identified with space shuttles . . .]

I eagerly identified with space shuttles; every day I lost a tile from my heat shield and anxiously awaited the consequences, but anyone who is lively and warm possesses so many defense mechanisms, unlike dead objects, or even the fireworks of technical ingenuity and NASA. The tile of my heat shield was always found by a girl who was worthy, because the first thing she did was press it to her heart, and then she turned it into a medallion. *It's amazing how many women wear so utterly mysterious a medallion, occasionally still warm.*

•

[In search of lost warmth . . .]

In search of lost warmth, I went to Hel to hear the stylish church services at Morgan's. You come to us today, Lord, universal and refined, as quiet as an oil slick on the Bay of Biscay. The sunflowers swoon like pirate flags in the still air. Dreamt once of spring; once of summer; fall. *And odds-makers—they predict, predict, and predict. I predict, you predict, the maggot predicts. And those singing above say they have a hot tip.*

•

[What good are all your considerable achievements now . . .]

What good are all your considerable achievements now, for example, your thesis on the density of the moment, which you defended at Utah's Far Out Institute, where you finally discovered unique conditions for isolating the moment from its broader impasse? How did that work out for you? Two grains of hard truth, less a pinch of autumnal dread, multiplied by the pulse of a man standing eye-to-eye with a naked star of the silver screen, plus the objectively complex movement from the motion of lifting, together with the yoke, as well as the revolving motion relative to the yoke in the planetary mechanism, that is, of the one degree of freedom that is now essentially the poetry of the absolutely present moment, comparable only to the swift exit from bar to rocky sea, which has frozen like lava at the gates of the town in this sleepy valley?

from
poemas
(2010)

SPRING ROUNDS

laughter by the river orangetip and lanterns
seraglios of lanterns and a stud earring
the cheerful "follow me" (swallow me) car
in the parking lot and the crappy fiat's back seat
and old pals who are dependably awesome
with their coke mandolin and pretzel rolls
and the smell of woodruff of bait under the awning
right after the rain to you alone i give
these veins of light and strands of shadow
a lump of hot earth a hushed whisper

to hell with your distant voice in the receiver
to hell with drops of dew on lilac
tears of alder above the mill what did you do
with that light the deutzia flowers charlock the view of delft
what was your last magic my make-up artist
the last vaginalia turned out so pale
followed by horrendalia that's now so-so
over the rainbow now making the rounds
there will be napalm for the poor napalm
is good if only it were still around

no one knew how much poetry we had in life
until we started to get a move on and love
people who run so fast sister
the satellite's ping will be with you always
the station's called cagliostro sister
just what do you think you're doing dave

i'm looking for point g in this hotel señoritas
i'm poring through treaties merged micro macro
3001 this odyssey is logical
3001 do you copy over do you copy

in the bandwidth from dada to three four left
in the hotel beds are burning check-out time
you can hear the sirens the water's about to come on
what's that trickling water at the door
what's that noise what's that *tumulto* it's nothing
and now we're heading for the spamhaus honey
from now on life is all about spam
3001 this odyssey is logical
3001 do you copy over do you copy
dormez-vous dormez-vous don't cry

in the entire complex just one senior
one director of operations and no security
the other seniors left for school
norm and annette will get into a fight
ziba will drink four beers in a sphinx
tunia and kalisia will play blackjack
goodson will go to town and get lost
bésame mucho fever love me tender
you cancan cancer marica and arnica
lolita and guernica augentrost

see nijinsky do the strandsky
o reel of celluloid o land my astronaut
jazz is paris and paris is jazz
we say bye bye moment you were lovely
humming *buh buh bum* faraway family friends

canoeing your time in the dormant uranium mine
fred and ginger body of the man in reno
marilyn and john f. dancing
reeling through niagara falls

to withdraw to one pole or the other
with a blush that'll melt any ice
a coup cooler than algida
you're holding a postcard cv portfolio
looking for work in the lethal vodka trade
lethe and vodka in a dark house of steel
you're looking for a job at lethal vodka
lethal vodka martinis
our application our supplication

in advance only abortion
euthanasia too late
of you we ask
something else

lemon bloody cola
something else

totus tuus sister
venus im pelz sister

the lethal's all done
the pop's all done
and now's an *all time low*
buh buh bum

DR. CALIGARI RESETS THE WORLD

innocently heartlessly and from a distance
doctor caligari recites the world
a little louder please
                         dottore
no point in sleep cesare
quick as a ghost the sun
came out shines is setting
no chance of getting sleep here

or else sleep cesare on such a night
and how much time do i have left dottore
and till the break of day cesare
(and you a little less than that alana)

we'll twist it till the first tear
till the first tears
till the first blood
till the "last" drop of blood

till the first *nothing!*
past the last something!
ha ha

holstenwall expo 2222
can I help you

today rome survived some scary hypnosis
berlin also survived its share of gnosis

moscow believes only in platinum sheen
oh my dear augustine
all of it serene serene serene

today the metro since morning filled with fog
in the fog many people on the platform
shining phantoms halo aureoles
polar specters in the metro hall
these pictures have gone all around the world
there are two trains at the metro stop
both of them take "to the air"
quick explosions rattle the surroundings
other stops "take" to the air
while they're hanging there you can watch them
from the pleasant remove from the superlight
these superlights it's their fault isn't it
no one knows how many stops we have left
someone says a dozen a mountain of a dozen stops
your stops hanna maria magdalena
there were a thousand stops in this city
today i spend hours on my way to the nearest
the stop called encouragement
the stop called elea

dreaming this i remember am i daydreaming
the event is serious wherever it happens
a kilometer out of town we couldn't find ourselves
the son fell by the road the girl went on recon
the professor disregarded "recon" and searched the luggage
rolls of paper towel three flashlights
without batteries thus the usual crap anyway and at night

you had to as our driver put it lose faith
was it the driver who gathered the cooker the tank the fish
the lecho the organist made such a fuss it's not so bad
we just have to get organized somehow

with each passing moment i have a greater sense of the weight
of light which seeks no cloud twilight dusk
no one will be able to find my dark glasses
which basically really worries me but not too much
didn't i lose the flute i didn't mislay the umbrella
what should i play on do i have tissue paper and comb
wanted to lead the light out like children from hamelin
hamelin vel hameln alias of holstenwall in turn
to molest them later in the cave or in the depths

and if the rat asks for our passports
we'll ask for the river of heraclitus for its depths its arrest
in the fluorescent cave where we will hang
injecting light into darkness or the other way around
whipping up a lot of romantic
dust *is that a friend or a fiend* driving us please
a rat named jagganath loves to dance
the lost as he shines a light on our passports
using "a limited set of means
he suffers 'finitude'" to the core

and for an encore rhymes "choir" with fsiorituras
it's worth a listen as the choir falls on its face and moans
maneuvered into this history it doesn't stand
a chance the bottom as he invariably calculates keeps
a stiff upper lip perhaps you too take your throne
on a triple rainbow our trio set out for the water tower

the professor had a catastrophic feeling
what tower what water *nomen omen* abolie
your low-pitched tent is on its way
your hard and anaerobic tent our mantra
sharanagamama is polish for gray naked lady

bless my soul the organist mumbled to the side
was it then that the bibliobus drove by
and from it the shot that killed you daddy
a bargain son because they only had a news roundup
and I passed pleasantly and it was an abyss
I died comfortably and it was an abyss
such as I won't say after four days
I spent a spell at a spa on cantharides
three hundred televisions in drywall
"enormous smoking crazy cities"
demolished hotels airports on fire
department stores rumbling in deflagration
your "promenades" helen marzena
the stations and arcades martha magdalena
over the city a storm like a vast cave-in
its tempestuous mayor tap-dances by city hall
nanking suffered some hard times today
sydney believes solely in morphine
everything's the next big thing

what they have in sherwood they have in lul woods
which still wants to remain here with us dear sir
this white squall of stars over my head
projects a silhouette on the brownish background of dunes
the swoop of wings like the noise of heavy water
hospital our driver shouted

now the wounded are piling up in stadiums
from above the spotlights (lux) the megaphones
here they have doctors for everything
there's a night shift and rounds
from above the jumbotrons (lux) the spotlights
wild fire kingdom timex show
rivers of fire flow through the water parks
these are now *de facto* and *de jure* fire parks
someone's mother has turned around into a pillar
of salt and no longer looks for her "loved ones"
no longer goes in for psychological counseling
cast me into the well and hang yourself *operation*
rotting sorcerer he's been murdered
the rotting sorcerer *has been murdered*
how beautifully heartlessly from a distance
dr charivari "recites" the world
a little softer please dottore

in a moment at the start of a trip in other directions
let's go to the kinds of places that never existed
a deep blue span like sapphire and steel
over the edge of the headland no quiet
no waves and that's where the seven seas are
our driver croons no dark cold ice sky and pebbles
no warm bright snow sun and clouds
nothing here speaks fluently with the glow of *fleurs de mal*

and we never went any further than the pier
behind us neon lights splendid excelsior elsinore
the stops filled with music those aquariums of orchestras
and the girls singing trionfi trionfi trionfi
does life still speak here in its own voice

o pen pen pen pen pen
we lost our connection or are out of range
lost star out of rage laughs the professor

i am writing to you place (or i'm not writing)
maybe you'd like to repent to draw aside
the crease in which you fall dutifully to pieces
"so-lavie di-le-jo whirlpooleddyfunnel
he-li venco-de-ho wellsandminetunnel"
and on in the kind of place that comes from everywhere
(shall come against him birnam wood
                              paranoia
                                   but what for)
place i'm speaking to you (or i'm saying nothing)
just try to curl up wither defoliate
disintegrate and scatter in all those directions
with the smile of a saint the whisper of hag
cast me into the well and hang yourself *operation*

with a bike on the ice at the mouth of the river
with a mirror on the ice at the mouth of the river

all my life crossways and seaward
all my life crossways and skyward

till the first *nothing!*
past the last something!
ha ha

holstenwall expo 2222
can i help you

the authorities are saying its spilloff
spilloff to a certain extent *fascinante*
big wheels are saying it's a stencil
a stencil of *ding-a-ling tremendese*
nasa announces it's schroedinger's cat
the vatican says it's voltaire's monkey

have you heard of voltaire's monkey
i have not heard of voltaire's monkey

over the city a storm like a vast cave-in
the tempestuous mayor tap-dances by city hall
the sandgrouse is a kind of spritely bird
the ermine is a notorious moth
(not to be confused with the lovely lady's ermine stole)
wild water kingdom timex show
what a strange lethargic trance
they're oxygenating the H2O

till all there is is h times two
                    ha ha

just h
        and π
"happy those for whom the fold
of"
szczęśliwi dla których fałd
ów

happy

POEMAS

i promised you poems and look what happened
what was there for us to write my monotonous muse
she wants to perform a biopsy of "my" voice
she has an ultrahypermodern device
and i have dark laryngitis joanna
i utter sounds like swollen notes
i stretch out poems like barbed wire
every implement speaks in its own voice
laryngograph spectrograph stroboscope spectrophone
that in inverse cancrine the seconds will go backwards
o all the instruments are saying in a single voice
that the day will not be dark cold quiet anything
night in time white sleepless and out of breath
aserejè ja de jè de jebe tu de jebere

•

please wait while we are completing your transaction
her hand on "my" knee is . . . breathtaking
take it slow i say my voice has so many layers
a hundred layers of scenic whispers and fissures
recesses stairs elevators there's the scaffolding
for works designers djs editors let's get to it
of this reality by the pontiff's grace of announcers
producers administrators (the world is up to
them)
> *now take leave of your senses and what's the night doing*
> *what's with this rule something's not right*

the sensitive apparatus says *pi pi* they sense the lights
the excellent instruments speak in a single breath
it would suffice for your to say *i love it i love it*

  •

what was there for us to write my repetitive muse
the night over time bottomless trivial and out of breath
the elegance of dream and blight mold swelling pus rust
a blossoming of fleur-de-lis *le wrist disconnected*
a breakout of *fleur-de-lis* from rotting wood
when the nightingales sing their lexicon to me at night
as i say there is love is that me speaking
to my love itself or is it to you
and she sees nothing we know nothing of love
but there's this tiny blog posted on the web
my profile shines prettily and pulsates on the web
my cv is an open book a letter of "interest"
i'm applying for a grant to perform a *coup d'état*
the night over time trivial sleepless and out of breath

  •

data transfer will be the *coup de grâce*
changing the speaker is dark territory
wilderness of whispers and sprechstimme
smoke ash and fairy tale choreographically
dreaming mechanically speaking oneirically
portentous dark arts nostalgic phrases
when i write "there's love" am i not waiting
for the parade of disappearing twins look

the visions are back confusing all the voices
i gladly volunteer to put some quiet sister to bed
tomorrow i'll run it in the papers an ad
for lethe it's in the euphony the basin of forgetting
tell me jehanne are we far away we've been going
for seven years we were faraway things

.

i run to you and fall so blissfully to pieces
my profile shines so prettily and flits around the web
bull's-eye metastases from the unconscious knots
of the eager syntaxes emitted in the blacks
of the screen are like a swelling of phantoms
of spectral tissue and the rusted scream in polymers
necromicine and neantizine sister
as gustaw digimorphs into konrad
in flares of acetone and bursts of void
further mutations without illumination
konrad jove meaning on a small scale
hey there but but
                    there are more details
in the original

.

*Next I develop these photos, tear them up, take the colors
and arrange new hues of varying intensity, from twitter-
ing orange to yellow infected with cerulean. Next I print
them on 100x150cm paper and start to draw on them
with paint thinner, lacquer, white-out, but a picture still*

appears, scratched out, and a picture that emerges in the
blurring of commentaries—of the poems inscribed in pho-
tography, such that all that remains is the illegible poten-
tial that blurred words are supposed to mean, what they're
supposed to describe.

•

on the right his star was returning to night
what was your last spell like my astronaut
my aquanautical muse what do you say now
the rise of capitalism parallels the advance of romanticism
and the individual is dominant until the close of the nineteenth century
the jungfrau sailed on rainbows like a spinnaker
on the hölderlin line from alps to sky
many rainbows have described her with garlands of flowers
another vessel had been named don juan or ariel
(a schooner sunken in a hurricane) and whoever
saw well knew that my girl and i cultivated
the cult of individuality without pause
on hydrofoils hovercrafts paragliders
we walked to the beach at dawn to follow the ravens
we found the pinkish-gray drowned man
(there were also *nomen omen* symbolic ravens)
the drowned man burned in a discrete fire
cozy cremation on the beach just me and you
we hummed *happy for those whom the fold*
of szczęśliwi dla których fałd ów *happy*
meaning folds of fire folds of water
or other exclusive special offers
me singing *quando quando quando*

and you singing *trionfi trionfi trionfi*
what would this world be without cheerleaders
in the desert o terrible spirit of surface
beautiful like a dreadnought in lightning
three oranges in an endless desert
(o pen pen pen pen pen)
on the wind and invariably *we all shine on*
like the moon and the stars and the sun

FALLEN LANGUAGE:
IN CONVERSATION WITH ANDRZEJ SOSNOWSKI

BENJAMIN PALOFF: The poems in your books are tightly interwoven: they speak amongst themselves and to each other, and at times you can even read them as a single monologue. If I am not mistaken, you have never published a selection that excludes any portion of what has appeared in the first editions. Does this English-language *Selected Poems*, then, tell a different story from the original?

ANDRZEJ SOSNOWSKI: Yes, it has to be different, because the selection changes and modifies the whole. And, of course, this is how it has to be, which is quite exciting for the author. As far as the "whole" is concerned, it's not that I feel an affinity with some concept of the Book, in the manner of Mallarmé. I just like when poems are in conversation with each other and at times extend certain threads, when they refer to each other, when they shift something within themselves. I also have the sense that, in an absolutely fundamental, almost physical (corporeal) way, the things I write are "telling" one story. *When all is said and done,* this will be one story. But only for me. Of course, changing the story is an unavoidable consequence of changing the language. You can't tell the same story in two different languages.

BP: But you're also a translator and a critic of modern American poetry in Poland. Is it fair to say that translating your poems into American English returns something to the place from which you yourself took it? That is, does it complete some aspect of your work? I wanted this question to sound more modest than it does . . .

AS: This is something that only you, and eventually your readers, can sense and know for yourselves. I have read quite a bit of American poetry, and I've translated some. Has some of that rubbed off on my own poems? I don't know. Let's take an obvious example. In "Poem for J. S.," there are moments in which I try to be in conversation with the form of James Schuyler's "The Morning of the Poem," and even with the poem's author. Does my poem sound like James Schuyler in English? I don't know. Sometimes this kind of return to the source, via another language, can recall a game of Chinese Whispers.

BP: I've always loved the name of that game in Polish: "Dead Line," or more literally, "Deaf Telephone." These days we usually call it Telephone or Whisper Down the Lane, but in Polish you know right away that the line is dead, that there's nothing to hear other than what you *want* to hear, albeit unconsciously. It sometimes seems to me that your poems, or even lines in your poems, are talking to each other while knowing in advance that the system of transmission can never work perfectly. As, for example, in your poem "Morning Edition": "Stop, / I think you misheard that." How do you go about creating this effect—an internal conversation that is truly dialogic, and not just a monologue in disguise?

AS: That's a tough question, because it concerns something that happens, as it were, spontaneously. The language that I feel within myself is a language that rarely goes silent, that rarely sleeps. And since it doesn't shut off and doesn't sleep, it usually speaks with itself. It is not, therefore, *my* monologue. It's not even the monologue of my own language, but a more complicated, polyphonic adventure, sometimes a dialogue, sometimes a polylogue. I really admire Elizabeth Bishop's poem "The Monument," because in it you can hear this beautifully illusory dialogue: you can hear at least two voices in two different registers.

BP: And to some extent this is something that American readers have come to expect from many of their own poets, though not necessarily from foreign poets. Many of the Polish poets known abroad are treated as unambiguous, even as moral authorities. I have in mind, for example, Czesław Miłosz or Wisława Szymborska. I should confess that I do not agree at all with that assessment, but I'm curious about the role this necessarily reductive way of thinking and reading plays in the reception of poetry in translation. And, to be honest, a lot of readers of poetry in Poland think the same way. How do you respond to those expectations?

AS: I'm not sure that I do—maybe I don't fulfill their expectations. *(Laughs.)* Let's go back to the earlier question. If someone has the same sense of the work of language as I have, I'll grant that it's very difficult for a poem to utter some unambiguous communication of a moral nature. Something like a "statement" or "message" simply cannot work, because some other voice always appears that suddenly challenges and dismantles the tone and composition of the ostensibly unambiguous utterance. I'll refer again to Bishop. Poems like "The Monument," "At the Fishhouses," "Over 2000 Illustrations," and "The End of March"—these are very serious, beautiful, and intelligent poems. And yet Bishop absolutely does not appear in them as a kind of moral authority. She stirs us and delights us, but she does not preach. In this case we can perhaps speak of artistic authority, even existential authority, but not moral authority.

BP: And which other Modern or contemporary American poets do you most enjoy reading? I didn't want to ask. Though the answers are often very interesting, the question is something on the order of "And the papers want to know whose shirts you wear."

AS: Ah, and now it's time to leave the capsule if I dare. Though I really am "floating in a most peculiar way." Are we talking about living poets? I don't have a thorough knowledge of many. I've been reading John Ashbery with great pleasure since the early 1980s.

More recently, I've been reading Cole Swensen with pleasure. Among my exact contemporaries I like Peter Gizzi, who also has occasion for some very interesting adventures in language. And I love the various styles of Harry Mathews, though he primarily writes prose.

BP: What you were just saying about language reminds me of Jacques Derrida, that "I have only one language, yet it is not mine." Though I'm not sure that we can ever "have" a language. Maurice Blanchot, whom I know you also admire—I'm thinking of your prose poem "Local Traffic Rules": "It was then that, in a manner as mysterious as it was inevitable, Maurice Blanchot became entangled in my sentences"—Blanchot was of a similar mind, that writing itself is an activity, whereas what we call "writing" is merely a trace of that activity. In this sense, is translation a trace of traces?

AS: Inevitably. But since you bring up such distinguished thinkers, perhaps we could also add Walter *nomen omen* Benjamin. I write in an utterly fallen, scrambled language, and it's possible that somewhere in this language of mine, in the language of these poems, there remains some fallen spark of revelation. And that's precisely what a trace is. You translate my fallen language into an equally scrambled and fallen American idiom, and your only essential task, "The Task of the Translator," is to discover and lift up this lost spark. *(Laughs.)* Besides, the translator is almost as lonely a creature as the author, right?

BP: Sure, but it seems to me that our very existence, as the process of identifying ourselves with an ideal—and here it's Jacques Lacan, not Blanchot, who's become "tangled in my sentences"!—means gradual isolation. Writing, and here I would include translation, is a treatment, and not an entirely effective one at that, for our solitude. Otherwise, what would be the point of all our letters, all our poems?

AS: I'd go along with that. Though there is also that aspect of living through your own solitude, a certain way of enduring the passage of one's own time, a certain way of listening to and hearing oneself. For me, this is as crucial as communication.

AFTERWORD

You can't live long with one word on your lips.
Even on the firing range or during the banquet,
as the wind carries scraps of dull rhythm,
the sergeant and the orchestra sink into themselves
without catching the melody in that which, like the echo
of vibrating strings—the filaments of the world—, unsettles them so.
This music from the center of the earth is also felt by women
stripped naked in the snow or summer gardens,
when, just before they're raped, their thoughts sweep
love's initial from the end of the telescope. The people
I'm talking about are leaving empty-handed,
tight as the knots of staves of stress,
dazed by the rain that compels them to say
they always wanted to live with but one word on their lips.

ERRATA

But of course the soul is the fifth wheel, to be
lost, not spared. Because the first violins
keep whipping up the chariots, gigs drawn
by hippocampi, deer, panthers, pigeons,
or some other phantasmagoric cemetery.
My dealer doesn't even want to hear about it.
New engine. Monotonous, the lap of life.

It'll just bedazzle you, *next year's* quota.
Man feels torn apart by models.
And when we transcribe ourselves this way,
for 102 voices, the wheels don't touch the ground,
our hair "soars to the Alps." Where the street
lets out, the duchess was dozing in her d'Aumont,
I drove up by *solitaire*, my rivals rolled up in a coach.

The arena shrinks. At the end, paradoxically,
a child under a lone spotlight rides in circles
on a unicycle. It's a marvelous picture,
a *Lehmhaus.* Music, the titles draw us aside.
I'd change just one word here. It should be: inventory.

A ndrzej Sosnowski was born in Warsaw in 1959. A poet, translator, and essayist, he studied and later taught in at the University of Warsaw. His collections include *Life in Korea*, *Nouvelles impressions d'Amérique*, *A Season in Hel*, *Convoy*. *Opera*, and *Zoom*. He has translated many American and English Poets, including Ezra Pound, Ronald Firbank, and Edmund White, and he has received many literary prizes, including the Kościelski Foundation Prize and the Kazimiera Iłłakowiczówna Prize.

Benjamin Paloff is the author of *The Politics*, and has translated several books from Polish—most recently, Marek Bienczyk's *Transparency*. He edits poetry and criticism at *Boston Review* and teaches at the University of Michigan. His poems have appeared in *New Republic*, *Paris Review*, and elsewhere.